Autumn of the Phantoms

By the Author

In the Name of God
Wolf Dreams
Morituri
Double Blank

Yasmina Khadra

TRANSLATED FROM THE FRENCH BY

Aubrey Botsford

The Toby Press

First English language edition 2006

The Toby Press LLC

POB 8531, New Milford, CT 06776-8531, USA
& POB 2455, London WIA 5WY, England
www.tobypress.com

Originally published as *L'Automne des chimères* (Éditions Baleine—Le
Seuil, Instantanés de Polar, 1998; Gallimard—Folio policier, 2002)

Translation copyright © Aubrey Botsford 2005

Copyright © 2005

ISBN 1 59264 143 1, *paperback*

A CIP catalogue record for this title is
available from the British Library

Typeset in Garamond by Jerusalem Typesetting

Printed and bound in the United States by
Thomson-Shore Inc., Michigan

Part 1

Chapter one

Of all the geniuses of the earth, ours are the most trespassed against. The poor relations of society, persecuted by some and misunderstood by the rest, their existence is destined to be no better than a dramatic flight from the vicissitudes of the arbitrary and absurd. If they don't die by the sword, they will die from being ostracized and despised. They will end up in an asylum or on a piece of waste ground, their heads crowned with thorns and their veins ravaged by alcohol. The only time they will rise to the level of news is at their own burial. Their only memorial will be a rudimentary tomb in the local cemetery, and their only glory will be that they had the good luck to have some talent at a time when merit rebounded only to those who were totally lacking in it.

Arezki Naït-Wali is a genius. He must be, because he holes up in a cul-de-sac at the very end of Bab El-Oued, entombed amid the shrieks of children and the dirty laundry of large families. Anywhere else, he would probably shine like a thousand suns. At home, he's a creature of the night.

A squalid building, a stairwell like a urinal, and the door of number 13, that opens on a shabby old man, trembling like jelly.

3

Arezki has the tragic face of Algeria's intellectuals. He's just a pale ghost with tortured hands and a pair of eyes to break your heart.

"How did you find me?"

"I asked the fundamentalists."

He smiles, and his nose, though flying at half mast, doesn't quite cover his mouth. He is falling apart in front of me, like a piece of decayed curtain fabric. If I had to choose between going to hell and uncovering the poverty I have just desecrated, I wouldn't hesitate for one second—for the peace of my soul—to accept eternal damnation.

"My housekeeper isn't well," he lies, to save face.

I can't think of anything to say to save mine.

My silence is embarrassing to both of us. He looks around as if getting his bearings, notices a bundle in a chaotic corner, picks it up furtively and signals that he's ready.

I nod and say, "I'll wait in the car."

We've crossed the city without noticing it. Me drumming nervously on the steering wheel; him hugging his bundle. The restless crowds on the pavements haven't once caught his interest, nor have the road hogs carrying out their appalling slaloms to get past us. He sits in his seat, composed, eyes glued to the windscreen, lips sealed. Despite the baking heat of the summer, he hasn't even thought to open the window. I don't know why, but seeing him like this makes me hate the whole world.

After an hour's driving, we enter the road to perdition—far away from the roads that have been secured, that is—and I hear him relax his grip on the bundle. I watch him out of the corner of my eye to see what he's going to do. I'm expecting to see him punch the dashboard or kick the floor in—but not the slightest sudden movement. Just his Adam's apple moving about in his scrawny throat and then, a few seconds later, his voice coming out in a pathetic gurgle, "Did he suffer?"

"Others have fared worse."

His breathing becomes irregular for a moment, then he regains control.

"I'm asking you, did he suffer?"

"He's not suffering any more now."

"Shot?"

"This isn't going to bring him back."

His hands suddenly grab the steering wheel and I'm forced to pull over on the hard shoulder.

"I want to know."

Angrily, I push him back into his seat.

"What do you want to know, Arezki Naït-Wali? Don't you read the papers, turn on the radio? We're at war. Your brother's dead, that's all there is to it."

He huddles around his bundle and goes back to staring at the windshield. For a whole minute, he tries to stop the tip of his chin quivering.

"I prefer not to find out at my village, Brahim. It's important to me that I know right away."

His sigh expresses so much suffering that my hand, of its own accord, goes to cover his.

I take my courage in both hands and say, "Sword."

It's as if I can see the explosion I have just caused at the core of his being. Slowly, he shrinks, makes himself so small that I feel I could hold him, from his head to his feet, in the palm of my hand.

"The torment!" he groans, throwing himself back against the seat.

And he starts weeping.

༺

The burial takes place at the old cemetery at Igidher. Many people have insisted on accompanying the deceased to his final resting place. They have come from the four corners of the land. Dignified elders, serious men, visibly traumatized youths.

Idir Naït-Wali could not be considered special. It was true that one of the greatest painters in the country was his brother, and it was true that his name raised his tribe to the level of nationhood, but, as a philosopher who was aware of the impertinence of vanity, he had chosen to be as worthy and discreet a person as his father, his grandfather and his ancestors had been before him; a shepherd by vocation, an unrepentant dreamer, an artist in his spare time and a warrior despite himself. Invariably to be found in the shade of an olive tree, his turban over his face and his shepherd's pipe within reach of his breath, he possessed twenty-odd sheep, which he loved to watch over as they grazed on a small patch of land on the way out of the village, and enjoyed the affection of his relatives. A true primitive because he was the real thing, he lived out his days as another man might tell his rosary, without making a fuss, without ideology, convinced that happiness—all happiness—was simply a question of one's state of mind.

The *imam* says, "The worst wrong one can do to God the Compassionate is to take a man's life. For in life resides His greatest generosity."

Beside me, Arezki wipes his hands on his thighs unceasingly. He is not listening to the *imam*, not noticing the birds singing their hearts out in the ragged trees. Every now and again, his stunned gaze comes to rest on his brother's white-shrouded body. Only then does he bring his hands up in front of his face and bow a little, exposing the frail and unkempt back of his head.

Arezki left at the first shovelful of earth on the remains. I followed him as far as the rutted road, then to the top of the hill where, as a child, he and his brother used to come and shout for echoes across the furrows of that region. He was there, resting his arm on the trunk of a fig tree; he had his head on the back of his hand, and thus forgotten himself for an eternity.

I don't know what to say. We stay up there, suspended between the sky and the earth, silent, minute, like two grains of dust. All around us, devastation stretches as far as the eye can see. I look at the parched orchards, the denuded hilltops and the ghostly rivers fashioning their own destruction. At the foot of the mountain, entrenched among its hovels, Igidher slowly decomposes in the sun, as mysterious as the ways of the Lord. My country is now just one vast agony.... I was born here, a very long time ago. Those days were known as the colonial period. The fields were so vast then that eternity, it seemed to me, began on the other side of the mountain. The wheat reached up to my shoulders, but I was hungry every day and I was hungry every night. Even then I didn't understand, but I didn't care: I had the good fortune to be a child. When the flight of a dragonfly made me feel I'd grown wings of my own, and my shouts of laughter mingled with the plashing of fountains, when I ran like a mad thing among the ferns, even though every stride created a mocking echo of itself, I knew I was a born poet, just as the bird is a born musician, and like the bird I lacked only the words to express myself.

I still don't understand. I just feel my way, in broad daylight. The laurels I have earned for my enlightenment are just blinkers. My prophetic gaze can't find its bearings. I'm not very proud of the adult I have become, and I await old age as another man might await the bailiffs, because nothing in the world makes me dream anymore.

𐦣

The night deposits its bile on the ancient land of the Naït-Walis. Before, this used to be a moment of enchantment. You could reach out and touch the stars. The patron saints of the *dechra** kept a watchful eye on things. All we had to do to reconcile ourselves with objects and creatures was watch the flame flicker to life on the wick of a lamp. Poor but not unhappy, clustered in enclaves but not isolated, we were a tribe and we knew what that meant. The fascination of faraway places, the mirages of the city, the symphony of phantoms— there was nothing to equal the tinkling of the bells around the necks of our goats. We were a race of free men, and we sheltered from the world, from its unclean beasts, its declarations and demonstrations, its investitures and investments....

Nowadays, our light is commandeered by the evening. The stars go pale with fright in the sky over Igidher. The unclean beast is present. In the silence of the *maquis*, it is preparing to ruin our lives.

"You're going to get hit by a satellite, Brahim."

I start.

Mohand sits down beside me, his rifle between his knees.

* *Dechra*: village.

7

"Come back to earth, my friend," he continues. "Whatever it is, it's happening down here."

He extracts a pack of cigarettes and offers me one. "Cigarette?"

"No thanks."

He flicks his lighter, sucks down three puffs in quick succession and blows the smoke out through his nostrils. In the distance below us, the village of Imazighen resembles a colony of fireflies.

I dig out a pebble with the toe of my shoe and kick it into the ditch.

Mohand turns to me and tries to catch my eye. His wine-laden breath blows in my face.

"Sniffing corks again?"

"The place doesn't smell the way it used to."

"What happened?"

"He was found in his garden, with his throat slit."

"Do you know who did it?"

"We don't need to look far."

"Why Idir?"

"He was there, that's all. For a few days, there had been reports of a group of predators in the area. They attacked the first person to turn up. It's their way of saying, 'Hi, we're back!' "

Mohand examines the enormous ash on the end of his cigarette, then stubs it out on a stone. The breeze ensures that the embers scatter among the bushes. We remain silent for a moment, listening to the stridulations of the night.

"Do you think 'they' are going to come back?"

"We're ready for them."

Once again, he tries to catch my eye.

"Is it going to last long, Brahim, this charade?"

"You're asking me?"

"Igidher isn't Algiers. We don't have time to understand around here."

"We don't know which devil to trust in up there either. It's a mess, Mohand, the biggest whorehouse in the world."

He strikes the ground with the butt of his rifle.

"What the hell are they doing, the people in charge?"

This time, I'm the one to turn to him. What I see in his gaunt face disturbs me. Mohand has aged considerably. The last time I saw him he didn't have a single white hair. Within three years, he's moved into full-blown decrepitude. He has more wrinkles than an ancient parchment and his eyes, once captivating, have become intolerable.

"In charge? Who's in charge? Are you talking about the puppets on the news, those cynical contortionists? In our country, Mohand, there are only perpetrators and victims. If you've got a problem, it's *your* problem."

My harshness shocks him. He gets up, grips his rifle angrily and leaves. I watch him go on his way, shoulders hunched, like a restless ghost.

I stand up too, clap my backside a few times to get rid of the dust and go back to the terrace, where the old men and some friends are keeping the inconsolable Arezki company.

ॐ

The chanting begins to wind down around midnight. One after another, the relatives leave the house on tiptoe, slightly ashamed to be leaving the painter alone with his suffering. Mohand is the last to leave. Before he goes, he approaches the photograph of the deceased hanging on the wall. The corners of his mouth tighten, probably to hold back a fit of rage.

He nods and says, "He was a just a *zawali*, a peaceful old man, much more interested in his sheep than the tumor growing inside him. I'm sure he didn't even defend himself against his murderers."

We both look at the portrait. A confirmed bachelor, he valued his independence above all else in the world. He was a kind of hermit, garnering his share of happiness in the tranquility of clearings in the woods. Now that he's dead, I ask myself whether he ever really existed.

Mohand looks at his watch. "It's time to go on patrol. My men must be getting impatient.... Are you sure you want to stay here?"

"Good night," I reply, removing my shoes ostentatiously.

"Okay then, I'll leave you alone. I'll post three or four men

9

nearby in case those maniacs take it into their heads to return to the scene of the crime."

I show him my big gun.

"We're ready."

Mohand nods and leaves, carefully closing the door behind him.

"Try to sleep," I growl to Arezki as I stretch out on the mattress.

I rest my pillow against the wall, punch it with my fist to make it more comfortable, slip my nine-millimeter under it and then put my hands behind my head so as to keep an eye on Arezki.

The mayor invited us to stay in his residence, but Arezki insisted on spending the night in his brother's hovel, among the antediluvian furniture, crude constructions of touching innocence, and his insubstantial memories.

"Maybe you'd like me to sing you a lullaby?"

Arezki looks at me long and hard.

"You have no respect," he sighs.

"Always looking on the dark side! Idir's sleeping, isn't he? Try to do the same. Because tomorrow, first thing, we're going back. I have no intention of hiring a crane to get you up."

Arezki is outraged.

"I won't go back."

"Of course you'll go back."

"My place is here."

"Hurry up and turn out the light, there's a good fellow. This dreadful bulb is getting on my nerves."

He turns out the light.

I pull the blanket up over my face, hug my knees and don't move.

There's nothing like darkness to comfort a man.

Chapter two

Back already, Super?"

Lino takes off his sunglasses and scrutinizes me with the air of a desert rat that's found a snake in its burrow.

"Did you hope I'd stay in the village for ever?"

"I thought you'd take a couple of days to recharge your batteries."

"Just admit it: deputizing for me has given you a taste for it."

Lino closes the door with his heel and collapses into a chair in front of my desk. He wipes his sunglasses on his shirt before putting them back on.

"How did it go at the village?"

"The way things are going."

"And your pal, the artist?"

"He's taken it very badly. I had to bring him back in a straitjacket. He would have made a perfect target out there."

"No incidents on the road?"

"We were lucky. Next time I'll take an escort."

"I see."

Lino examines his fingernails, frowning. Suddenly, his lack of enthusiasm intrigues me. I realize that something has happened during my absence.

I push the telephone aside so as to catch the lieutenant's evasive eye. He turns away and pretends to be interested in the official notices plastered on the wall.

"Go ahead, make like there's nothing going on," I say encouragingly. "I can take it."

He purses his lips. He wrings his hands for a full five seconds, unable to work out where to start.

I lose my patience:

"I've only been away two days. You're not going to make me believe I've missed a crucial moment in my career in such a short time."

He summons up the strength to face me.

His voice trembles, "You don't know?"

"That depends on what."

"There's an envelope, marked for your attention, in the boss's office."

"The way you say it, it sounds like you're talking about my own burial permit."

"That's almost what it is."

I can feel my guts twisting themselves into knots.

Lino goes back to tormenting his fingers. His cheekbones are twitching, and his olive-hued lips are quivering in an unattractive manner. Suddenly, the telephone rings, paralyzing me from head to foot. As I pick up the receiver, I notice that my hand is shaking.

At the end of the line, the director's whining voice nearly finishes me off.

"Brahim?"

"Yes, Director."

"Got a minute?"

"Right away, sir."

It takes me two attempts to hang up properly.

Embarrassed by my discomfiture, Lino undertakes an examination of the defects in his cheap sunglasses.

"It's started," I mutter.

"I'm afraid so," he says apologetically.

I pick up my jacket and walk off down the corridor. People move aside as I pass, as if I were a funeral procession. I don't need to turn around to know they're crossing themselves.

From the second story on, my legs fail me. I have to grip the banister to carry on climbing. I did prepare for the worst, but now that it's here, I'm in a panic.

The director has lost weight. Three days ago he was fit as a fiddle. I deduce that he has been hauled over the coals.

His colorless face aggravates my dismay.

Distantly, he indicates a chair with a weary gesture. I sit down in an armchair, my throat dry, my ears burning.

"You're up the creek, Brahim," he says pompously. "And I don't know the paddle that'll get you out of it."

I try to frown, but can't. My vocal chords are in danger of shattering at the slightest murmur. I content myself with folding my hands somewhere and awaiting the storm.

The director picks up a sheet of paper and more or less throws it in my face. I grab the piece of paper in the air and skim it without understanding what it says.

"You've been summoned to see the big cheese," he says helpfully. "You have every chance of being skinned alive."

I gulp convulsively.

He adds, his voice heavy with reproach:

"You're as stubborn as a mule, Superintendent. I did warn you."

"Will that be all, sir?"

"Isn't it enough?"

I put the piece of paper back on the desk and stand up.

He stands up too and accompanies me to the door. Once there, he grips me by the shoulder and says confidingly, "I don't know whether it'll be up to me from now on, but I want you to know that I don't let my guys go easily."

I nod and leave, feeling as though I'm unravelling as I walk down a corridor with unsettling perspectives.

13

Chapter three

In Algiers, the moment you leave your own office or slum you're in hostile territory. Don't try to educate the taxi driver, don't hope to soften up the bank clerk, don't push the doorman—it's a miracle he's even noticed you. Wherever you drag your depression, you feel like a leper. Nobody welcomes you with any consideration. Nowhere is there a smile to cheer you up. What you are entitled to, however, is the same abrupt, peremptory "Yeah?", the same frown that immediately strips you so utterly bare that before you risk entering an establishment you find yourself hanging up your dignity in the cloakroom and exercising your pride at doormat level because, wherever you fetch up, it's best to keep a low profile.

So when I enter the square in front of the Ministry of the Interior I know what to expect and stoically accept the arrogance of the sentries, then the hostility of the security guards and finally the contempt of the underlings.

After having been gone over with a fine-tooth comb, I'm hustled into a sort of dungeon where I am ignored for hours without a cup of coffee, without a word. There isn't even an ashtray to have a smoke. Mustn't let it get to you. It's a low-ceilinged, windowless hole, two meters square, painted a dull grey; enough to make an animal chase its own tail until death overcomes it.

The chief of staff doesn't deign to remember my torment until I've started to simmer like a stew in my cheap security guard's tunic.

"This way, Mister Llob," a secretary says with the inviting courtesy of an executioner showing a condemned man to the scaffold.

A door the height of a tower opens onto a vast room lined with trophies, coats of arms and enormous paintings. In my mind, this is a trapdoor gaping over my ruination. I nearly sprain my ankle on the carpet. Not because of the hard-packed dirt I drag my feet on all day long, but because I'll never get used to the quagmires of the higher echelons.

Mr. Sliman Houbel is enthroned behind a control center covered with telephone gadgets, calling cards and impressive-looking files—because it's important to make visitors believe that a senior official always has a lot on his plate and isn't shirking his responsibilities.

He begins by undoing the knot of his tie, then spreads his bird-of-prey wings and sits meditating a moment, like a god who doesn't understand why the world he created is getting away from him.

As for me, I don't flounder about too much. Every time I'm up before a superior officer, I have the irritating feeling I've made a serious mistake somewhere. Despite a reputation for being more or less honest, a sense of guilt emasculates me and I catch myself making myself small, or rather, radiating humility.

Mr. Houbel looks at me and senses an internal weakening; he takes his inspiration from it and, without offering me a chair, pushes a book toward me.

"What's this, superintendent?"

I swallow but can't clear my throat. After a titanic struggle I hear myself squeak, "A book, sir."

"You call this fecal matter a book?"

This time, my Adam's apple starts playing tricks on me. It jams against my palate and won't come unstuck.

Sliman Houbel curls his lip as unselfconsciously as a donkey raising its tail. He looks me up and down for a long time, uncertain whether to spit on me or wipe the floor with me.

"Do you seriously take yourself for a novelist, Llob?"

With the tip of his carefully manicured finger, he pushes my work* away from him as though it were a piece of garbage:

"This grotesque pamphlet is unequalled except by the lowness of its author. In striving to ridicule your society, you've only managed to reduce the scant respect I thought I had for you."

"Sir…"

"Silence!"

A fleck of his spittle hits me in the eye.

He stands up. His well-fed frame towers over me, putting me in the shade. He's the boss. And among us, power isn't measured in terms of ability. Its true unit of measure is the degree of menace it exerts.

A light flashes to his left. He presses a button and roars into a microphone:

"I'm not in for anyone, Lyès. Not even the Raïs."

The Raïs, no less!

The floor shakes as he comes round his desk to examine me up close. He can douse himself with Dior all he likes, but still his breath nearly overcomes me.

"I hope I'm not telling you anything new when I say that the class dunce would identify your scribbling as belonging to the anal school of literature, Mister Llob. Your literary excursion relies more on meticulous masturbation than any real intellectual conviction. You don't even deserve to be called a scribbler."

Now he's really telling me. That's one of his prerogatives.

Among us, even if you're a great warrior, if you're hierarchically inferior you're supposed to be inferior in both stripes and brains. Your talents owe it to themselves not to get ideas above your station.

I look at this despot: a mean little specimen of this republic of tsars; young, rich, his shoulders broad enough to receive all the manna heaven has to bestow; never in danger, never in want, every

---

* *Morituri*, by Yasmina Khadra, *The* Toby Press, 2004

finger in some pie or other, a suite in every grand hotel and feet made to step on you.

And I, Brahim Llob, a monument to loyalty but a giant with feet of clay, senile at fifty-eight years of age, sometimes a platform and sometimes a stepladder, spending my nights in unheated jalopies and my days at the shooting range, I stand there at attention, allowing myself to be dressed down like a dog, I, who gladly risk my life every day God gives me so that puffed-up and ungrateful hypocrites can continue to hold sway with impunity.

Sliman Houbel has time to notice a speck of dust on his shirt. He moistens his finger with the tip of his tongue and embarks on a laborious cleaning operation, like a lunatic.

He mutters, "The Minister has requested me to transmit to you the utter disgust he felt upon reading your latest pot-boiler. If it weren't for your many years of service and your record in the resistance...."

"Mister Houbel," I burst out, overcome. "Why have you summoned me here?"

He jumps, does the chief of staff. His eyebrows meet in the middle and his nostrils quiver like an ant's nest.

"What do you think, superintendent? Why do you think you're here? Did we gather our rosebuds together or something?"

"That's my point."

He realizes that I'm beginning to recover, and is a tiny bit disconcerted.

To avoid my eyes, he taps the book:

"Why this filth?"

"It's not filth."

"Yes it is. Real filth, with the added ingredients of impropriety and stupidity."

"I report to you as a policeman, not as a novelist."

"Silence!"

Another millimeter and his flecks of spittle will be blinding.

I've heard artillery firing; Sliman Houbel's shouting has considerably more effect: the dissuasive effect of abuse of authority.

He sniffs noisily to contain his rage. His eyes are about to leap out at me.

"Let me remind you that you are a civil servant and, as such, under an obligation to be discreet. We have authorized you to publish your foolishness in the past, but we cannot tolerate deviancy of this kind. You've gone too far and you've brought a whole lot of trouble down on yourself. Nobody would like to be in your shoes, not for all the tea in China."

His crimson complexion makes his features intolerable.

"Your whatever-it-is is infamous, disgraceful. I always knew you were just an out-of-touch phrase-maker, a fanatical scribbler, but it's a long way from there to believing you capable of such bullshit!... I'm sure—naïve as you are—that you don't even realize the effect of your fantasies."

Whitish foam thickens and stretches at the corners of his mouth, and his bad breath fills the room, contaminating even the corners.

"You can't assume you have the right to criticize your superiors and drag your country through the mud just because you're an incompetent, frustrated malcontent. You're well placed enough to know what's true and what isn't. Of course we make a mess of things from time to time, but we do it by omission, not commission. The country isn't quite on the right track. If it's heeling a bit here and there, that doesn't mean it's capsizing. Like all young nations seeking good health, we're condemned to experience setbacks and to be the object of tactlessness. That's how we learn. All the great powers followed the same path. Their merit lies in having had the strength to overcome the obstacles, to accept..."

The trouble with people who raise up totems is that they think they can use the same tree both to hide the forest and to warn off poachers.

"Sir..."

"Shut up! You have neither the weight of a martyr nor the makings of a hero, superintendent. You're way beyond the absurdity of your characters. If you think we cut a sorry figure, try to breathe a little of your righteousness into us: maybe it'll help us pick up the pieces and start again. We are an exhausted people, disoriented, disappointed. We would be unhappy if our elite consisted only of defeatists.

We need to believe in our star, to bathe in its light. Criticism doesn't blow us away. Our changes of mood won't allow it."

He notices that my book has turned to shreds in his hands, nods like a sultan faced with the ingratitude of his eunuchs and subsides abruptly.

"I feel sorry for you, superintendent…the Secretary has also requested me to inform you that you are retired, effective as of today.… And now, get out of my sight."

Since a boss's schizophrenia doesn't excuse mutiny, I click my heels, turn and get ready to leave.

"Superintendent!"

I turn round.

He points his finger at my chest:

"Don't get too big for your boots, as they say."

"That's one of my own favorites, sir."

He looks as though he's stepped in some dog mess.

Chapter four

Not until I find myself on Rue Larbi Ben M'hidi do I remember my car, which I left behind in the Department's car park. I have to commandeer a taxi to go back and get it. Once behind the wheel, I realize the extreme gravity of my solitude. Mina and the kids are still at Bejaïa, my few friends have other fish to fry and, my discomfiture growing, I find I can't summon up the courage to pick up my stuff from the office. Suddenly, Algiers seems as unfathomable as a parallel universe.

I drive and drive through the white-hot streets, my eyes staring, my head empty, deaf to the racket around me, unable to get my bearings.

"Are you colorblind or something, you moron?" a truck driver yells, pointing out that the traffic light has turned to green.

His voice reaches me through an infinity of filters. I get tangled up in the gear shift and stall several times. During the time it takes me to sort things out, the light turns red again. I shoot off at high speed, letting loose a frightful chorus of horns and curses.... *Don't get too big for your boots...*says the voice in my head.... *I warned you,* follows another, nasal one.... *Shut up*.... The voices follow each other round and round, jostle each other, besiege me, hammer at my temples, oppress my very soul.... *The way you say it, it sounds like you're talking about my own burial permit.... That's almost what it is.... The secretary has also requested me ... disgust....*

A squeal of tires: I wake up with a woman two centimeters in front of my bumper. She looks at me with huge eyes and hurries across the street, her bag of shopping clutched protectively to her chest.

Night overtakes me on the sea front, slumped on a boat ramp, pursuing my thoughts among the lights of the port. A police patrol I didn't see arrive silently fans out around me, machine pistols poised against the slightest sudden movement. A sergeant shines his flashlight in my face and asks for my papers.

"You can't stay here, superintendent," he advises me. "A suspect vehicle has been reported in the area."

"What time is it?"

"It's getting late. Go home."

I thank him and go back to my car.

Just as I reach the door of my apartment, the telephone starts ringing. I hurry without knowing why. Dine's hoarse voice greets me sharply at the other end of the line: "I've been trying to get hold of you for ages."

"News travels fast, I see."

"Especially bad news. Where have you been?"

"Licking my wounds in private."

"I don't like to hear you talk like that, Brahim. I rely on you to keep a cool head."

"I'll go and put it in the fridge right away," I promise.

"Can we meet tomorrow evening? I'll be at the En-Nasr café from ten o'clock on. If you think hard times are what friends are there for, at least you know where to find me."

"That's kind of you."

I hang up.

As I take off my jacket, I realize nothing has passed my lips since morning. I find some bread and cheese in the cupboard, make the necessary coffee and go into the living room to torment myself some more. I sit down in an armchair in front of the window. Through the grimy panes I can see the heights of the city suspended in limbo. Algiers isn't a place for night owls any more. Her nights are haunted. Her evenings don't believe in soliciting moody insomniacs, and don't inspire trust in those who are adrift and easily swayed ....

The clinking of crockery wakes me up. I have dozed off in the armchair. Lino is there, on the sofa beside my chair, sipping a cup of coffee and watching me curiously.

"How did you get in?"

"Easiest thing in the world: you forgot to shut the door."

"Great!"

He puts his cup down on the low table and leans forward to look at the rings under my eyes. He is drunk as a lord.

"If they ever kick you out on the street, I'll hand in my badge," he says as a gesture of solidarity.

"I can't afford to pay a driver."

"I'm not worried on that score. Talent, competence, integrity— they're out of date. The only criterion for promotion they've left us with is intrigue. And I'm not going down that road."

Lino isn't thinking about what he's saying. He's my disciple. I've brought him up in accordance with the *sunnah** and the recommendations of certified *ahadith*.† If he's letting himself go like this it's because he's in pain. It's his way of expressing defiance.

I push him away gently and go and get changed.

When I come back, I find him standing with his nose pressed to the window and his hands clasped behind his back. I go over and tap him on the shoulder: it's time to lie to him a little, make him believe that Brahim Llob is tough, that he'll triumph over adversity. He turns round to see what he can read in my eyes. He frowns in alarm. I realize that the expression I'm killing myself to put on my face must be somewhat lacking in conviction.

---

* Sunnah: way, custom. The sunnah of the Prophet Mohammed is the second source of Islamic law after the Qur'an.

† The *ahadith* (pl. of *hadith*) is a body of teachings of and stories about the Prophet Mohammed.

"What are you planning to do?" he asks, with a lump in his throat.

"Think."

"Should I conclude that you want me to leave you alone?"

"I'd be proud of you."

He looks at the tips of his shoes.

"This business has taken me by surprise. I don't seem to be able to handle it properly."

"It's not the end of the world, Lino."

He nods.

"You know you can call on me any time."

"How could I doubt it?"

He salutes, hesitantly, and leaves.

※

As I do every time I come adrift, I find myself steering a course for Da Achour. He's my own private sedative. I find him on his veranda, sprawling contentedly in a rocking chair, his shirt open over his elephantine belly and a straw hat pulled down to his ears. When he sees me turn up, looking defeated, he leans over to turn down the radio and hastily gets ready to welcome me.

I sit on a stool beside him and my eyes flit among the white-flecked waves. The beach is crowded. The shouts of children chase those of the seagulls across a healing sky. A few young swimmers, in an attempt to catch the eye of the girls feigning indifference from the shade of their umbrellas, venture out far beyond the breakers, serenely ignoring the lifeguards' panic. On the rocks, fishermen stand among the geysers of spray, striving to catch stubborn fish with rod and line. This is the Algerian summer: it has its highs and its lows, but it's determined not to make any concessions. If I had to lay down on canvas the essence of life itself, there is no question but that it would have the colors of this lull in hostilities.

"I was expecting you yesterday," says Da Achour, hardly moving his lips.

"So you know?"

"There are no secrets any more. You look like a photocopy of yourself."

He raises the brim of his hat indolently to examine me.

"Are you all right?"

"I suppose so."

"Good. The stagnant waters of the pond have never succeeded in altering the purity of the water lily."

"But they don't turn it into a wreath, either."

"It has no need to be a wreath: its majesty is enough on its own."

I nod.

He adds, "I was worried about you."

"Did you think I'd put a bullet in my brain?"

"You're so unpredictable."

A large ball lands near the veranda. Two fearful kids come and get it, watching us out of the corners of their eyes. My smile chases them away faster than the bogeyman's scowl.

"What do you think? Have I been a fool?"

"If you doubt yourself, it means you're not worth a fig."

"I don't."

Da Achour takes his hat off completely and twists painfully round to face me.

"A poet doesn't do foolish things. He exposes the foolishness of others. Naturally, that makes some people resentful. I've read your book. It's worth it. Trust me."

"They've thrown me out. After thirty-five years of hand-to-hand combat with idiots. Thirty-five years of putting up with all kinds of irritations, of believing religiously in order, principles and loyalty despite the lies, the power-mad maneuverings, the dirt. I was going to take early retirement, but then this damned war fell in my lap. I thought to myself: a good man doesn't leave the ship when it looks like it's headed for the rocks; he has to regain control, come hell or high water. And then, one morning, they show you the door and order you to disappear, just like that, without any consideration at all...."

"That's because *they* don't know what *they're* doing. The world is divesting itself of its poetry. The simple beauties of yesteryear don't appeal any more. There's no drama except in failure, no faith except in investments. Men don't have consciences any more, just obsessions: cash–dough–loot; cash–dough–loot; cash–dough–loot…. They're certain that their fundamental values depend only on the barometer of the stock market. That's why the death of an intellectual, the burning down of a library or the murder of an artist upsets them much less than a bad investment."

"If I understand you correctly, I have to become one of them."

"Not at all. That's precisely where you intervene."

"As a party-pooper."

"The poet doesn't need arson: his suffering lights enough fires for everyone. Your book has it right. That's what matters above all else. The rest: the problems, the arguments, the threats—in fact, all this stressful arm-waving you talk about shouldn't put you off. This ghastly war has at least this in its favor: it reveals us to ourselves first of all, and then to the rest of the world. The masks are off. Everyone is in his element. The demagogues invent to the point of absurdity, the intriguers intrigue shamelessly, the carrion eaters don't have to pretend the flesh of their brothers is from the delicatessen, the monsters that were dormant among us parade around the boulevards. And then, above this stinking mob, there's *you*. You tower over your world, like a god, and that's fantastic. If you hadn't dared to shout your anger and disgust from the rooftops, if you had kept quiet and allowed these bastards to give free rein to their fantasies with impunity, I would have been terribly disappointed."

His jowls suddenly flush:

"Lose this hang-dog look, Brahim, and do it now. Can you tell me whether a single one of the thousands of victims paving the roads of our retreat deserved to be disemboweled like an animal? Among these hordes of nihilistic cannibals, can you show me a single one who deserves to be forgiven? You have nothing to reproach yourself with. They showed you the door, but a thousand others will be opened to you, mine first. You have carried out your duty to the full. You have *succeeded*. The sons of bitches know it, and they're trembling. They thought they were the more cunning, they thought theirs was the perfect crime. But perfection comes from what is right, only from what is right."

He stops, out of breath, eyes staring and lips foaming, and collapses into his seat. His chest is heaving, and his eyes quarter the undulating sea. I can't hear the shouts of the children or the sound of the waves; I hear only the creaking of his chair as it starts rocking again. I stand there for two minutes, suspended in a bubble, as if I had just been hit on the back of the head, and then I come back to earth. Da Achour's serenity fills me with a kind of relief. I am suddenly aware of the breeze stirring his shirt, the branching delta of sweat around his navel, the fine shadow around his eyes, and the casual dangling of his arm which, like a sign, advises me to think more carefully.

"Thank you," I say.

Chapter five

If you're not glad to see me, tough luck," says Dine as he sweeps into my home like a tornado. "I waited for you at the café for two whole hours, and you didn't come. I said to myself, two and two makes four: either that idiot's gone and committed hari-kari in his bath or I'm not his friend. I came over to find out which."

He brushes me aside with his hand, inspects the bedrooms and comes back to hustle me about in the hallway.

"No obvious fire," he reports. "No overturned furniture, no smashed tiles. That shows you're holding up, and I'm glad of it…. So," he continues, spreading his arms, "are we going to stay here short-cir-cuiting our neurons or are we going to get something to eat?"

Without waiting for an answer, he picks up my jacket off the chair and shoves it into my arms.

"It's depressing, your place. Let's go out and have us some fun, let's go paint the town red."

I start making polite noises. His bruiser's fist propels me out onto the landing.

"Oh, do get a move on; otherwise we'll miss the star turn, darling."

In the twinkling of an eye, I find myself out on the street.

Dine pushes me into a big shiny car, hurries to get behind the wheel and shouts, "Like my wheels? Makes you sit up and take notice, doesn't it? You thought I'd be sitting around telling my beads all day and scouring the honky-tonks all night, didn't you? Wrong! Retirement is the start of a new life, an amazing change. Thoroughbred stallions die of orgasm, my dear. Old age is for nags and donkeys."

Dine's enthusiasm ends up relaxing me a little. I sit back in the seat and take a deep breath. The car speeds silently over the tarmac. In a sky studded with millions of sparks, the moon struggles to grin like a Cheshire cat. I close my eyes and let the wind from our passage ruffle my hair and puff out the collar of my shirt.

Dine takes me to the Coral Sea, a luxurious restaurant sprawling over four hectares of gardens criss-crossed with paved avenues and wrought-iron lamps. The sea is right next door, with a slice of beach from the Garden of Eden and some sculpted rocks. A few couples walk about on the fine sand, laughing loudly but taking advantage of the dark areas between spotlights to fall silent for a moment. We park the car in the lot and attack a reception area that glitters as fiercely as the monumental chandelier hanging from its ceiling. Behind his dark red mahogany counter, the receptionist adjusts his bow tie before granting us a worrying professional smile.

"Good evening, Mister Dine. It's a pleasure to have you with us this evening."

He presses a button. Some kind of wading bird appears immediately from somewhere, stiff and haughty.

"Is Mister Dine's usual table ready?"

"Yes, sir."

"In that case, I leave him in your hands."

"Very good, sir."

The flunkey obsequiously points us in the right direction and then walks ahead of us, neck stiff over a plain frock coat, nose like a hook stuck in the air.

"Where did you import this antique from?" I whisper in Dine's ear.

Dine digs an elbow in my ribs to make me keep quiet.

The flunkey leads us to a table with flowers on it, beside a bay window, helps us into our seats and then vanishes as if by magic.

"Retirement seems to have done you proud," I comment to Dine.

"Seems that way...."

"Have you gone into business?"

"The only thing I collected during my career was enemies. Some friends remembered favors I did them. They asked me to manage a small food-products business and I didn't look a gift horse in the mouth."

I glance around the room and recognize a few *nabobs* showing off their harems, officials engrossed in negotiations with foreign counterparts and then, at the back of the room, the villainous face of Haj Garne,* sharing a table with Soraya K., the local madam. They're both looking me up and down, disdainful sneers on their lips.

"Do you remember Kader Lawedj?" asks Din, discreetly pointing out a stunted but obese little man on our left.

"He's become a heavyweight."

"In both senses. Word is, he's the next head of the Committee of Heroes."

I nearly swallow my false teeth.

"Is this a joke?"

"It sounds like one, but it's practically official."

Well, well, well! I came to know Kader Lawedj when he was on national television, training in the waffler's art. An unusually abject bootlicker. He would entertain high officials in the studio. On those evenings, the nation found it had to flick endlessly from channel to channel or else implode. Those who didn't have satellite dishes simply turned their little screens off. So when he was up as a candidate in the elections to the legislature, he ran away with all the votes. The people had no choice. It was the only way they could prevent him from ruining their evenings. But it wasn't long before Lawedj, honorable Member of Parliament, went back on the air. In less than a year he headed five national commissions before getting

---

* See *Morituri*. Toby Crime, 2004

tangled up in a sordid story of influence-peddling and the misuse of public funds. The gentlemen of the press were all over him like a pack of hounds, devoting their front pages to him for weeks on end. The poor bastard went from one courtroom to the next, and from scandal to depression, and then dropped out of sight. The storm blew over and he reappeared with an astonishing *mea culpa* cooked up by a team of corrupt journalists. Then they did him the signal honor of giving him a bowel-loosening telethon to front—all in order to reha-bilitate him–then fixed him up with a job as mayor of a quiet little village. Two years later he came back on his dashing white charger, as founder member of some phony political party.

Lawedj catches me looking at him, raises his glass in greeting and then pays no further attention to me. One thing's for sure: this guy will go far. He has an inexhaustible supply of shamelessness and he knows that the fewer scruples you have in a baroque system like ours, the greater your chances of making it to the upper echelons. Once you're up there, there's nothing to choose between you and the gods. The most appalling characters are described as merely unusual, and notorious acts in the past are presented as glorious feats of arms. When you have money in one hand and power in the other, heaven hardly counts for anything.

"Stop staring at him like that, you'll annoy him."

I sit down.

The waiter comes to take our order, then leaves.

I catch myself watching Lawedj again, his Paris suit, his smooth cheeks and his subdued gestures. *He's nothing but a crooked piece of shit*, I tell myself. *Glossy on the outside, stinking on the inside. Mustn't be envious of a piece of shit.*

A woman makes a magnificent appearance in the room, her head wrapped in a futuristic scarf. As tall and thin as a maypole, she's squeezed ferociously into a gorgeous robe open all the way down to the rise of her buttocks. She stands among the tables for a moment, her little bag against her tits, waiting majestically for someone to at-tend to her. A flunkey hurries over, begs her to follow him and seats her at the table next to us. Dine smoothes his moustache, as if on cue. The woman thanks the flunkey, directs a barely perceptible nod at us, clasps her pink hands under her porcelain chin and loses herself in contemplation of the frescoes adorning the ceiling.

"Just look at that masterpiece!" cries Dine feverishly. "Madame Zhor Rym, the most beautiful widow in all Algiers."

"I know her."

"Do you really know her?"

"I just know who she is."

He falls onto my shoulder:

"Will you introduce us?"

"You have a wonderful wife, Dine. I'd be sorry if you forgot about her."

He balls up his napkin in his hand, pulls his carcass away and sulks.

At the other end of the room, Haj Garne catches the flunkey's eye, whispers something to him and stands up. He goes round the table to pull out Soraya K.'s chair. The former donkey trainer's gallantry almost knocks the table over. Soraya looks daggers at him and leaves the table like a grand lady. The bewildered Haj Garne first checks that his neighbors haven't noticed anything, and then hurries to catch up with his companion.

Soraya swishes contemptuously past me. Haj Garne, for his part, pauses to greet Dine and then takes an interest in the collar of my jacket, "I was delighted to hear that you'd been thrown out, Llob. Now I can almost begin to have a bit of respect for the police."

"Anything to please you."

"It certainly does! I relish it every time I think about it. Llob out on the street: that's what I call happiness, don't you?"

He spreads his arms in a gesture of absolute beatitude.

"It's marvelous," he rejoices….

"Have you given up your dinner on my account?"

"You don't miss anything, do you? I thought the place had been disinfected."

He rubs his hands. His rough palms give off a disgusting smell.

"So, just like that, you're calling yourself Yasmina Khadra now? Honestly, did you take that particular pseudonym to seduce the jury for the Femina Prize and distract your enemies?"

"It was to pay homage to the courage of woman. Because if anyone in this country has it in spades, it's the women...."

He sniggers, which makes his face frighteningly ugly.

"You know what, Llob? You've been taken in by some transvestite."

"Are you coming or what?" yells Soraya from the stairwell.

Haj Garne asks her to be patient, pulls out a business card and puts it on my plate, "You never know, do you? Anyway, if you need a job as a night watchman, call this number. I own two disused warehouses on the way out of the city."

He looks at me sidelong for six seconds and adds, "Shit! Am I happy today!"

And he rejoins his whore on the stairs.

"I appreciated it very much," chirps Madame Rym, her chin resting on her fingernails and her eyes fixed stubbornly on the ceiling.

Neither Dine nor I understand whether she is talking to us or thinking aloud.

"I beg your pardon, madam?"

Her enormous, virginal eyes deign to come down to my level.

"I said I appreciated it very much, Mister Llob. And I'm referring to *Morituri*."

"Very kind of you to say so."

"I'm not in the habit of listening at keyholes, but that oaf was doing everything he could to be overheard."

"That's because he's a bit hard of hearing."

"Losing his marbles, more like."

"Don't worry yourself on that score: he never had any."

She unravels her fingers and turns her face toward our table. Her divine neck turns in slow motion, with hypnotic grace. The woman is a marvel. The refined style of her outfit and the elegance of her movements add an inexpressible something to her remarkable beauty, the something that differentiates the canvas of a master from that of a forger.

"Won't you join us, Madame Rym?" suggests Din.

"That's very kind of you. I'm expecting someone.... In any case, Mister Llob, if the wind should blow you toward Hydra one day, I'd be delighted to see you. I've always wanted to talk to you. I love writers."

"We shall be sure to come and visit you, madam," Dine promises in a surprisingly musical voice.

"I'm giving a little party on Monday. Nothing extravagant; just a get-together for friends."

"We wouldn't miss it for the world," Dine pronounces solemnly.

"That's settled then. Monday, from eight o'clock on."

She smiles and goes back to contemplating the ceiling.

The conversation is over.

ə€

Trousers around his ankles and tie over his shoulder, Kader Lawedj is washing his hands in the bathroom. Already in an advanced state of intoxication, he is finding it difficult to control his movements. He passes his wet hands through his hair and then over his face. As he straightens up, he sees me in the mirror. The sight of me makes him uneasy again.

"*Bon voyage*, douche bag!" he says, as I push on the door of a cubicle.

He turns, swaying, and waves bye-bye uncertainly.

"And good riddance."

I pay no attention to him and go into the cubicle.

When I come out, I find him in the same place, standing at the sink, knees trembling, on the point of collapse. He wipes his hands on his tie and tries to take a step. The weight of his backside drags him backwards, and he ends up with his ass against the wall.

"You forgot to flush yourself down the toilet, Sam."

"You've got the wrong man, pal. My name is Llob, Brahim Llob."

35

His finger wags no, and every flabby inch of him moves with it:

"You are Sam. And you belong in the gutter. You're going to shove yourself down the toilet and then flush, or else I'm going to do it for you."

"I'm too fat."

He snorts fit to split his nostrils and roars,

"You bastard! You piece of shit! You asshole! Can't you think of anything better to do than make fools of us in front of our enemies? You think you'll get a laugh out of the cheap seats like the sold-out clown you are, is that it? If the country disgusts you, get lost. Go join the gangs of bastards and deserters across the water."

He hasn't got the wrong man. Kader Lawedj is aiming directly at me. It seems as though he's regurgitating the indigestible sediment left in his guts after reading my book. His purple face is trembling with ungovernable rage, and foam is beginning to ferment at the corners of his mouth.

He staggers, leans on the sink and points at the mirror behind him.

"I bet the mirror would smash at the mere idea of reflecting your image. You're disgusting, Sam. You're a pile of shit like no other. Algeria will recognize her own. As for the traitors, they've got it coming to them: they'll get it up the ass, in public."

"You should put a little water in your wine, Mister Lawedj."

"Up your ass, more like. It hurts when it's dry. You're just a vulture. But you've picked the wrong carrion. Algeria is a land of nobility, an impregnable sanctuary. And Algerians, the real ones, they're aristocrats to a man. They stand up straight in the face of disaster. They don't know how to bend. No force, nothing will bring them to their knees. We are an invincible race, Sam. If the lightning bolts of heaven don't dare to strike us, your ridiculous little book isn't going to unseat us. You fool! You sad bastard! You imbecile!"

He spits at me. But he's too drunk, and the gob of saliva sticks to his lips and dribbles pathetically down his chin. He leans against the wall, gathers himself together, collecting his strength for an enormous effort, catapults himself toward me and attempts a punch. I dodge him. His momentum leaves him sprawling in a cubicle. He grabs the toilet and struggles to lift himself up; his shoes slip on the tiles and he falls down again.

He's pathetic.

"You're finished, Sam. We'll have your hide, you traitor, you sell-out!"

I leave the rest room.

His drunkard's voice pursues me:

"Finished...You're a dead man, you piece of shit...."

᠅

But that's not the end of my surprises. After dinner, the manager of the Coral Sea intercepts us at the reception. He starts by shaking Dine's hand, ostentatiously withholding his own so as not to greet me, licks his lips several times and says, "Mister Dine, our establishment is open to you at all times. We consider you a particularly valued customer. However, I would be grateful, in the future, if you were more careful of the company you kept. This is a private club. Our members are very particular. And we have our reputation to consider."

"What's the matter, Mister Abbas? Does my friend's face piss you off?"

"If that were all there was to it, I wouldn't give a damn."

Dine looks at us in turn, jowls quivering. He clenches his fist and starts trembling threateningly.

"Let's go," I say.

"Just a minute," he rages, removing my hand from his arm. "What are you insinuating, Mister Abbas?"

"I think I was clear enough."

"Perhaps, but I didn't grasp it."

The manager snaps his fingers. Two gorillas, straight out of a freak show, appear on the spot.

"Would you show these gentlemen out, please?"

The two gorillas seize us before we can come up with a rejoin-der, hustle us to the exit and throw us out. The manager looks at us contemptuously for a moment; then, in a tone of voice that gives us pause, advises us never to set foot in the place again. Before turning his back on us, he says to me, "Every little thing aspires to grow, Mister Llob. But dwarves don't get the chance. For them, growing is all about getting old. But they have to live an awfully long time."

Part II

The true horror is to know you're behaving
like a fool and not care.

Brahim Llob

Chapter six

The doorbell rings, and I'm thinking about something Lino said to me one evening on the coast road. We were in a grill room, having a bite to eat. Lino, his chin streaming with juice and his cheeks bulging, made the following profound observation: "The most sensible way to serve a cause is not to die for it but to survive it." At that time, the country felt good, I had nationalistic fervor coming out of my ears and, inveterate zealot that I was, I wasn't in the habit of paying attention to the remarks of subordinates. It comes back to me today like a boomerang, and has the effect of a truth that comes out of the mouth of a child. I've been chewing it over for hours, and I still can't digest it. It's terrible.

All my life, I've been missing the point. I've been a bear with a sore head, much closer to caricature than to the forest, and the relentless baseness of my surroundings has kept me in a state of what you might call savage megalomania, blind to some and deaf to others, disgusted to see my fellows trotting happily behind a cardboard carrot. Now I *know*: all that grayness that used to veil my face, all that corrosive hostility that used to gnaw at my guts—it was because I wasn't *listening*. I heard only the bitterness of my own incorruptibility;

saw only my brutish rejection of everything that didn't conform to my innermost idea of values and principles. Perhaps I was trying to protect myself from the surrounding wickedness, or to dissociate myself from the activities of the crooks who were so fashionable in the centers of power, and found the best possible alibi in my cocoon. Utopia! Once again, I hadn't understood a thing.

Of course, I would comfort myself that every trashcan contains something that's intact. But, I would react in desperation, so what if something's intact, if it's in a trashcan? Whether it's salvaged by a scavenger or ends up on the trash heap, it hardly escapes its destiny in the world of garbage…. No, that's not true! Maybe it can be recycled!

Today, I'm certain that the stagnant waters of the pond do not alter the purity of the water lily.

I had a choice of two ways to do my duty in society: *to be its servant or its master.* I chose the one that still seems the less wearing. It was hard, but I don't regret it. I'm still asking myself questions today. Should you take your ideals to the limit, or change sides? And what is the limit? The firing squad, the ambush, or just the mosque with all the other old men, as befits a good pensioner?

Lino was right. His mouth was full that evening on the coast road, and not just with kebabs. Dying is the worst thing you can do for a cause. For there will always be a race of vultures hanging over the ruins and the sacrifices, cunning enough to pass for phoenixes. They won't hesitate for one second to use the ashes of martyrs to make fertilizer for their Edens, or the tombs of the missing to make monuments of their own, or the tears of widows as water for their mills. And I can't abide that. Perhaps that's why I took so long to answer the doorbell.

"Have you mislaid your ear trumpet or what?" roars Dine on the landing. "I've been ringing for a good ten minutes."

Seeing my grim expression, he turns the volume down and proffers a toothy smile. Then, with a nicotine-stained fingernail, he taps his watch to tell me we're going to be late for our appointment.

Reluctantly, I take my proletarian jacket off its hook and join him at the foot of the stairs.

Dine is hopping up and down with excitement. He has put on his Sunday best and some Italian shoes and has splashed on enough cologne to make a decomposing corpse seem approachable. In order to look serious, he has encumbered himself with an enormous pair of horn-rimmed glasses that take up half his face.

"Listen, old friend," he says as he opens the door, "if you're going to keep up this sullen act for the rest of the evening, we'd be better off staying at home. Let me remind you that we're visiting a lady. So make a few adjustments, because you're being a total drag," he adds, closing the door behind us.

I have absolutely nothing to say the whole way there. My bitterness seems to contaminate all the joys of the earth, Dine's above all. Nor does he find it useful to play the fool in an effort to force a smile out of me. Gradually, my foul mood overcomes him, like a baleful fog. After a while, I'm ready to ask him to pull over and let me walk home. Not to exercise my legs and mind, but just because I think Dine's beginning to piss me off too. After all, I have a right to stay at home, do some housecleaning in my head, step back a bit so I can see where I stand. What does Dine know about *my* loneliness? Why is he taking me to see a widow I'm not necessarily glad to see again?

If he fancies her, that's not my business.

In a sense, Dine is using me.

I haven't had fun at parties for a long time. It's one after-effect of a childhood that was taken from me, then of a youth I missed out on, and I'm not likely to get them back, not the way things are now at any rate.

When I was a kid, there was always a sheet of glass between happiness and dreaming of happiness.

At the Guillaumets' farm, where I labored as a handyman, I didn't have time to enjoy myself. I was torn between errands and domestic chores, and I devoted myself to deserving every penny I earned, accepting my highs and lows philosophically, like the swallows, which can admirably reconcile the whiteness of their bellies with the blackness of their backs.

God made rich and poor, I was taught.

So when my employers' house was decked with garlands, when carriages and cars turned up, backfiring, from the four corners of the land, when the hubbub spread up the mountainside and women's laughter reached the heavens, I would content myself with a branch of a tree or a patch of shade and watch the happiness of others as if they were fish in a tank.

I would stay like this, chilled to the bone and yet amazed at the same time, my nose pressed against the sheet of glass, until the morning, and I never for one moment harbored resentment against the people of Igidher because they didn't light up my child's eyes.

In those days, it was always the colonials that had something to celebrate. That's how it was; you had to live with it. That's why, to this day, wherever there is joy I immediately find myself on the sidelines.

We reach Hydra forty minutes late, because a pitched battle between the police and a gang of terrorists made us turn back.

Mme. Rym lives in an impressive manor on the corner of Rue de la Paix, facing an oasis-like square ringed with palm trees. The place seems quiet. No cars parked on the pavement, no noises. A group of vacant teenagers under a mimosa tree, their complexions cherry red. Some of them have heads shaved to the temples, others have ponytails; all of them show a shiny ring in the left ear. In Algiers, this community is known as the Brotherhood of Daddy's Boys. They're quite capable of walking across a war zone without even noticing.

Mme. Rym is relieved to see us turn up. She was beginning to despair, she confesses, as she takes my arm to introduce me to her friends, who are apparently quite at home amid the surrounding splendor. There are girls, pretty as embroidery, ladies like stuffed turkeys, elegant gentlemen. Here and there, no doubt chewing over their good fortune, old ladies wallow in sofas with the timeless haughtiness of sacred cows, pretending to be indifferent to the charms of gigolos who are willing to get personal for a bit of pocket money. Further on, the cream of society. Among others, I recognize Baha Salah, an industrialist with seismic powers: he has only to blow his nose to cause an incident. Amar Bouras, a shameless regionalist who had the good sense to be born into the right tribe and follows to the letter the motto of his kind: *get rich quick and rule for a long time*. He heads a mafia-like political party. Dr. Lounes Bendi, a legendary intellectual and inveterate opportunist, who wouldn't hesitate to shoot his own mother down in flames if it would get him talked about. Omar Daïf, a fallen film-maker with a stubborn squint, who is often to be seen begging for charitable sponsorship at cosmopolitan gatherings. Sheikh Alem, a passionate apostle of sedition in '92 and proud of his six months of internment, learnedly sporting his subversive beard the way a porcupine sports his quills. And, of course, the inescapable Kader Leuf, an upright, objective, perceptive and incorruptible journalist universally considered to be as piquant as a French cheese.

We go from *nabob* to dowager like an eighty-year-old taking on an obstacle course. One gentleman is so busy interrogating himself that he can't spare us a single second. Which goes to show what a deadly serious undertaking it is. Between pretended courtesy and furtive *salaam-aleikum*s, we manage, more or less, to complete our tour of the cattle market, at the end of which our hostess abandons us to take care of some new arrivals.

"Unbelievable!" says Dine exultantly, devouring Mme. Rym with his eyes.

"The opulence?"

"The lady, what do you think?" he snaps, annoyed.

I give him the benefit of the doubt and file the information away.

Mustapha Haraj quits networking and clinks his scotch on the rocks under my nose. Haraj is a banker. We got to know each other during an interrogation he's not about to forgive me. Stunted as a milestone, sinister and nasty, he's more likely to take on a risky loan than smile at a stranger. Utterly and completely loathsome!

"Am I hallucinating, or what?" he barks with his gut-scouring voice. "Brahim Llob among the elite—who'd have thought it?"

"Your enthusiasm gives me comfort."

His whole face expresses outrage.

"I have no intention of giving you any comfort. If you only knew how sick you make me feel…. Unfortunately, words fail me."

"That's not all that fails you, alas!"

He looks me up and down, just before the *coup de grâce*. He stirs his potion in a lofty manner and adds, "I have a friend in Paris. I'll ask him to check whether a gargoyle's gone missing from Notre Dame."

"Don't trouble yourself. There's one within spitting distance."

That shakes him from top to toe. His veins bulge horribly around his bald pate. Suddenly, a massive explosion rocks windows and walls, interrupting the conversation. Taking advantage of this ill-timed incongruity to beat a retreat, Mustapha Haraj swiftly rejoins his fellows on the terrace. A long way away, a gigantic plume of smoke shows the location of the drama that has once again befallen the city.

"Seventy-eight," sniggers Sheikh Alem, unable to hide the morbid glee shining in his eyes. "That's the seventy-eighth bomb to go off in Algiers."

I go over to the balcony to watch the tentacles of flame lashing at the skirts of the night. In the frozen silence, the bearded one's giggling takes on funereal proportions. Of its own accord, my hand grabs him by the collar of his robe and pushes him to one side.

"I beg your pardon...."

He tries to frown. My fingers close around his neck, causing him pain; he retreats, reduced, clothed in the baseness of a smooth-talking, cowardly fraud, and his retreat creates a strange kind of brightening of the light, as if a demon has been exorcised.

A few minutes later, the wailing of sirens reaches us in an apocalyptic chorus. A woman painted like a Japanese actress joins her bejeweled hands in melancholy prayer, seeking in the heavens an interlocutor who might be willing to take her seriously. Behind her, a young couple exchange disconcerted grimaces, probably fearing for their evening.

"Let's not stay here," Baha Salah says in response.

"You're right," Amar Bouras continues. "Why let a bunch of vermin make our lives complicated?"

A few guests join the industrialist in the main room. Those that remain hang about in the courtyard, listening to the distant sounds with varying degrees of attention.

Doctor Bendi lights his pipe with Olympian calm and then, one hand in his pocket and the other around his symbol of peace, contemplates the cloud of smoke as one might contemplate a work of art.

"God! We hide this war like a shameful disease," sighs Omar Daïf. "I feel as if I'm going mad."

This doesn't distract the intellectual at all.

The film director clenches his fist. His wrinkled features are even more expressive of his dismay.

"When will it all end, doctor?"

"I've left my crystal ball at the office."

The doctor's tone is dry and brisk.

Omar Daïf loses himself in his thoughts and then resumes, tormented:

"If there's an escape from prison, a bomb, a gunshot anywhere else, the whole country is mobilized. The smallest incident gets a statement from the president the very next minute. Here, young girls are raped and beheaded, children are maimed by bombs, whole families are hacked to pieces every night, and we behave as if nothing's going on."

The doctor takes a long puff on his pipe, blows the smoke in the film director's face and rejoins the *nabob*s in the salon.

Omar Daïf turns to an old lady beside him:

"But it's true. I know, let's check the television. Turn it on and you'll find a report on our tragedy broadcast from the Antipodes."

Grandma frowns at her courtesans first, as if wondering why she, of all people, should be accused of anything, then wrinkles her nose and disappears, her flock of gigolos at her heels.

A condescending Kader Leuf intervenes, taking the film director by the elbow. "Let's not be too dramatic. Our war must be seen in the context of the deviancy to be found on every continent. It's in the nature of things. We're no different. There's Zaïre, Rwanda, Bosnia, Chechnya, the Middle East, Ireland, Afghanistan, Albania.... What's happening here is biological, basically. Our country is learning about itself. It's going through puberty. This is just an adolescent crisis."

I find myself alone on the terrace, slumped over the balustrade, feeling a bit faint. Mme. Rym glides up beside me. Her hand rests lightly on mine.

"Why did you invite me to this circus of assholes, Madame?"

"For you to see what I have to put up with every week."

"You didn't have to."

"That's why. I'm trying to make some other friends."

"Really?"

"Absolutely. In my world, people only talk about profits, politics and alliances, never anything else. I'm tired. I'm a dreamer, Mister Llob. I like to forget myself on the banks of a river, close my eyes and believe in fairy tales to the point of kissing a toad on the mouth. Sometimes, I just want to shut the door and go and recreate the dream behind the bushes. I'm a country girl, Mister Llob. My father owned a cabin a stone's throw from the forest. We moved because he was afraid I'd get robbed at the foot of some tree. That's all I used to do: wander about in the woods."

By now, her fingers are intertwined with mine. Her eyes are shining like jewels in the reflected light of the streetlights. Her perfume is markedly stronger than the scents of the garden.

"I'm like those roses I tend with such devotion. None of my guests notice them. The only reason they all come is to have a good time. And when they leave in the small hours of the morning, I have tears in my eyes like the dew on my flowers."

She takes me by the waist and I can feel her breasts pressing against my side.

"Come, my friend, it's time to sit down for dinner."

I follow her.

"Do you like flowers, Mister Llob?"

"Among other things."

"Do you have a preference for any particular flower?"

"Let's say I pine for the one flower I'm not likely to pick again."

"And what's that?"

"The flower of youth."

⁂

Dinner is served in an enormous room with velvet carpets. The banquet is spread out on a table at least twenty meters long. There's enough to feed a whole tribe for two days. I am shown to a seat between two playful ladies at the center of the arrangements, Mme. Baha Salah on my left and Mme. Haraj on my right. We are graced with the presence of Amar Bouras at the head of the table. I would have been surprised to see anyone else. Since he thinks he's at a conference, he spouts forth an incomprehensible speech asking us all to join his movement to re-establish peace and prosperity in Algeria, in massive numbers. His political staff clap. This is the signal to attack: we launch an assault on the soup.

"Which party do you belong to, Mister Llob?" asks my right-hand neighbor.

"My own family, ma'am."

"Quite right. I don't see your wife here."

"She's at home, running my bath."

"You secretive little fellow. While she's running your bath, you're trying to find a pretext to justify it."

A second explosion shakes us. Baha Salah promptly takes control again.

"Pay no attention to those morons, dear friends. Let's stuff ourselves until we throw up."

The industrialist's confidence relaxes the atmosphere. Lying in wait behind a fat Hausfrau, Sheikh Alem is keeping an eye on me. The moment I turn my head he calls out:

"Seventy-nine!"

"You should be ashamed of yourself, Sheikh," says the film director rebelliously. "A *haj* like you, one foot in the grave. You're happy to see your country go up in smoke...."

"It's the military's fault," yaps the one with the beard. "They shouldn't have intervened in the election."

"The military did its duty. If the German officer class had shown the same courage and blocked Adolf Hitler, there would have been a civil war in Germany, but the world wouldn't have gone through the Holocaust, the mass deportations, or the ovens."

"Starting a world war has never been part of our agenda," the sheikh protests.

"What about the cultural purge the FIS* was proposing? And intellectuals being promised the gallows? And the totalitarianism everybody could see coming? If they'd won, I'm sure the country would have experienced genocide on an unprecedented scale. Thank goodness they made the tactical error of opting for civil disobedience...."

At this, Dr. Lounes Bendi taps the side of his plate with a spoon to make everyone shut up. With infinite concentration, he considers the sheikh and the film director in turn, a withering smile on his lips.

"...Raise the tone, gentlemen. We're not in some corner café here."

Certain of having brought the house to order, he puts his spoon down and leans back in his chair. Two of his fingers fiddle with his Lacoste tie.

Beside me, Mme. Baha Salah starts trembling like a sow in heat. She has not stopped staring at him since we sat down at the table. And every time their eyes meet, she shakes from head to foot.

The doctor takes a deep breath and roars, "How is it that the FIS, which was about to win the legislature hands down, turned into outlaws, from one day to the next? What was the point of their civil disobedience? They virtually *were* the Parliament. So why did they chuck it all away, just like that, and end up in jail?"

The doctor's questions go all round the table: no takers.

"It's true," a short-sighted spinster pipes up. "It doesn't make sense. People were cheering for them in the streets. The polls gave them an eighty-percent majority, with or without gerrymandering."

"It does seem strange, when you look back on it," a gigolo agrees, mainly to attract attention to himself.

The doctor realizes he's raised the bar too high, as his smile shows.

He says, "This civil disobedience story doesn't stand up. It was just the first of the fabrications. The FIS were unveiling a crash pro-

---

* FIS: *Front islamique du salut* (Islamic Salvation Front).

gram. They'd been refining it for years. The FIS didn't come to rule, but to wage war. The elites were caught on the hop. Their corrupt wealth went against their socialist façade and was beginning to show them up. They were afraid of being swept away in a tidal wave of abuse and speculative deals. They needed breathing space. Quickly. It was infuriating to have to prop up overseas banks and leave billions of dinars lying idle. They wanted to get their plunder back, invest at home, in this country, a real Eldorado lying fallow. But there was a catch. Every time the people heard that such-and-such a big shot wanted to get some big project going, they would look down their noses at him, 'Where does his money come from?'—'*Min 'ayna laqa hada?*'—would be the word on the street. In the end, it was essential to take it down a peg or two, this populace that was standing in the way of progress.... But how? War, of course! They needed a crisis, an honest-to-goodness, shit-a-brick crisis, but a manageable crisis.... Play the Berber card? The stakes were very high.... The Arabization card? Intellectuals make poor mercenaries. So it was necessary to blow the place up, scorch the earth, traumatize people's memories, help the opponents of progress see reason, starve this population of wrong-headed and ungrateful scroungers to the point of begging for bread to feed their kids and prostituting themselves for work of any kind. And then the elites say, cynically: 'I'd love to invest, but people insist on gossiping'—'To hell with gossip! Who cares where you inherited your fortunes from? Take the derelict factories and build empires out of them. If you're not keen on clearing up the mess, we'll sweep right up to your front door. All we want is work.' And that's the way the trick is played. Simple as a farce. And while the theoreticians follow the scent of phantoms elsewhere, the nation burns. The firefighters who offer to help are one and the same with the arsonists. They drew the right card: fundamentalism. The brothers were available, drool-ing with frustration, belligerent, indoctrinated. Yesterday, they were cultivating their hatred. Today, they're entertainers. You don't teach your grandmother to suck eggs. The negotiations to give official sanction to religious parties had the sole aim of legitimizing sedition. The Islamist movement was raised to the rank of prophecy, and then thrown on the scrap heap. Naturally, the victims of this con took up arms. First the MIA,* the FIS's armed wing. Then the GIA,† the Iron Fist of God. This war is just a work in progress, carved up in an amicable way by the political-financial mafia. When the foundations of their empire have been laid, they'll snap their fingers and calm will descend, like in a dream. The poor taxpayer will be so relieved he'll never dream of demurring again."

At this point, he pushes his plate away, stands up in the deafening silence, puts out his pipe and leaves bravely, without a glance at his audience.

We sit there, dumbstruck, for three minutes, guilty of falling short of a monumental intellect. Mme. Baha Salah's knuckles are white with the effort of crushing her napkin. Opposite her, Dine can't quite catch his breath. Everyone looks at everyone else, and no one dares say a word. In the end, I am the first to show a sign of life, by taking two sips of water: in the bottomless silence, they resonate in my throat like the evening's two bombs.

"Pure fantasy!" cries Kader Leuf at the end of the table.

"Yeah," growls Baha Salah. He fancies himself as the Nero of erudition.

"Goebbels was right. Any time a man gets out a book, you should reach for your revolver," sniggers Haraj.

"The hell with these intellectuals! They think they're so clever, that's why they've been taken in," says a substantial fellow with a forehead like a battering ram. "Honey, do me a favor and pass me that silver platter over there."

"These eggheads, though—I mean, really! You just have to see them crucifying themselves on the foreign TV channels. They can't help being sacrificial victims. They're afraid, they sleep badly, they're being hunted, they can't go get their cars out of the parking lot, people are trying to kill them, they're all alone, they're fighting on all fronts...."

"The things people do for a pathetic little visa!"

"Careful now," comments Amar Bouras. "It's worked for some

---

*   MIA: *Mouvement islamique armé* (Armed Islamic Movement)
†   GIA: *Groupe islamique armé* (Armed Islamic Group)

of them. I used to know this wretched little pen-pusher who had to sweat blood to put two sentences together. Now he's one of the luminaries. He walks away with all the prizes, every time."

"If you ask me, these Westerners are all a bit crazy. Just tell them you're condemned to death and they feel guilty."

"Condemned to death? What do you mean, condemned to death? The poor bastards being hacked to pieces in the street, in the villages, in front of their children, were they condemned to death?"

"*Astaghfiru Llah!*"* sighs Sheikh Alem, his neck swallowed up by his shoulders.

"...Listen, folks," says Baha Salah irritably, gesturing expansively at the mounds of food. "We're here to joke around, but let's not go too far. Let's forget these dogs, please."

"They're not going to spoil the party anyway," adds Haraj.

All hands descend on the plates in choreographed spontaneity, all mouths mutate into hatch covers, the clattering of forks spreads throughout the room, punctuated with the sound of sucking.

"This salmon is really succulent," simpers a vamp, licking her fingers voluptuously.

"Madame Rym," says a playboy from beneath his golden locks, "may I say that your *crème anglaise* is exquisite."

"Queen Elizabeth made it for me herself."

Laughter, and the page is turned on Doctor Bendi and the bombs and miseries of the world.

Mme. Baha Salah takes advantage of the racket to leave on tiptoe.

My neighbor on my right seeks out my leg under the table.

"You're not eating, Mister Llob?"

"I'm watching my weight."

Her hand teases my knee, spreads out on my thigh, enjoying itself on it from top to bottom. Her forwardness takes me by surprise. Her poker face disarms me. I stiffen. She translates this into consent and continues her journey through regions normally considered taboo.

---

* *Astaghfirou Llah!*: God forbid!

"No use venturing any further, ma'am. The starter button in my navel's been under the weather for years."

"I'm very skillful, you know. I can take care of that in two minutes flat."

"I don't doubt it, but it won't be necessary."

She removes her hand and puts it back on the table. Without relaxing her smile, she looks at me for a long time and confides:

"You're incredibly sexy."

"It seems that way, darling. I'm actually a bit like a melon. My gut expands at the expense of my stalk."

Upon which I throw in the towel and stand up. "No hard feelings, ma'am?"

She winks: Fair's fair.

A disapproving Dine catches up with me.

"Really, you are impossible. What's the matter now? Can't you stay anywhere for one second?"

"I want to go home."

"I'm making a deal, for crying out loud!"

"I'm not stopping you. I'll get a taxi."

"Out of the question. We came together, we'll leave together. Look, help me out, dammit! You'll only be depressed at home anyway. Just give me an hour."

"Half an hour, Din. I won't hold out a minute longer."

"Very well."

"Isn't there anywhere I can be pissed off in peace? The sight of this gilded rabble is torturing me."

"There's a library. Go down the corridor until you get to the hall and it's on your left. Go in there and sober up a bit. There are some fabulous books, a giant TV and a video."

I nod and go to the hall. On my left, a huge padded door gives onto a room the size of a gymnasium, cluttered with leather armchairs, silverware and endless bookshelves crammed with books. I light a cigarette and start looking for an interesting writer. Just as I plump for Naguib Mahfouz, a moan catches my attention. I turn round. The room is empty. Another moan leads me to a small door, hidden behind a mini-bar I hadn't noticed as I came in. I walk over to it, glance through the keyhole and see, sitting in an armchair with his widespread legs framing a splendid erection and his elbows on the armrests, Doctor Bendi and, at his feet, Mme. Baha Salah frenziedly tearing her clothes off while administering dizzying fellatio.

I can't take it any more.

Chapter seven

What are you, jealous of my good luck?" Dine complains, driving like a maniac. "I was this far from closing the deal of my life."

I let him rant to his heart's content. My thoughts exploit my melancholy, enlarging the abyss that is inexorably sucking me down into its darkest depths. I don't feel the need to cling on any more; worse still—I feel a kind of inner peace as I allow myself to be swallowed up, the stuff of this life having become abhorrent to me. What was I looking for at Mme. Rym's? What was the point of that repellent, vulgar display of imbecility? Do I have to get used to the idea, once and for all, that nothing stands up in the face of cash, that anything can be bought and anything sold, *absolutely anything?*

I am horrified.

My third cigarette in less than fifteen minutes fails to asphyxiate me for good and all.

Dine runs a red light, and the tires screech as he takes a tight curve. He's beside himself. His fist pounds the steering wheel and thumps the gear shift. His circus act barely distracts my attention. The vehicle bounces into a pothole as it goes round another bend, sending me crashing into the window. Dine doesn't notice. My sudden departure from the home of the most beautiful widow in all Algiers hasn't gone down well with him, and he's trying to vent his rage by furiously crushing the accelerator pedal.

"You can't seduce destiny with that gravedigger's mug, pal," he rages. "Hurry up and get your portrait retouched by some beautician. Frankly, I despair of you."

I'm the one who's despairing, though. Despairing at the sight of my world wilting under the exhalations of phantoms; despairing at the realization, at my time of life, that nothing remains of the hopes I struggled to entertain in the face of adversity and the Hun-like advance of opportunistic and greedy arrivistes. Oh, Dine! What happened to those carefree years when you used to do the most extraordinary acrobatics to make ends meet? What became of that proud young man whose pauper's salary had no effect at all on his rectitude? The bait was tempting, it must be said. It was all too easy to "do like everyone else," to carve out a place in the sun, to peddle your influence in return for a steady income; it was within reach of every purse, and naturally the city started reeking of decay. But there were some who chose not to betray the oath of honor, nor to exchange their principles for illusory privileges. They kept their honor rather than a fortune; they remained upright in the midst of darkness.

My fourth cigarette takes me back twenty-seven years, to a small police station in El Hamri, a poor quarter of Oran. I turned up there one April morning, my suitcase in one hand and my papers in the other. It was raining cats and dogs that day, the sky was terrifying. I was on assignment, and already I felt out of place. I was discovering a city I didn't know. There was a cheerful fellow behind a rickety desk. He couldn't speak without punctuating his sentences with gales of laughter. His smile gladdened the storm outside, all by itself. His name was Dine. We became friends at the first handshake, and we stayed friends for years after, despite the vicissitudes of a wretched profession. But some tough facades, it seems, crumble abruptly at the slightest touch.

We arrive in front of my building. The avenue is deserted. The few feeble streetlights lined up along the sidewalk look like ghosts that have been reduced to begging. A wan glow surrounds their tips with a depressing halo. The days of yesteryear have gone. The hoodlums who used to raise hell in the doorways have disappeared. The shopkeepers lower the blinds as soon as night falls. Then the street is given over to the throes of uncertainty, idle winds and stray dogs.

"Move your fat carcass," scolds Dine. "Life is a choice: double or quits."

"What's it worth, d'you think, twenty-seven years of friendship, tax free?"

My unemotional tone surprises him, literally strikes him dumb. First he releases the steering wheel, then he leans back against the door and faces me. His moustache quivers.

"I beg your pardon?"

"What game are you playing?" I ask him point-blank.

He doesn't understand, but he can clearly smell trouble.

"What is this nonsense, Brahim?"

"What game are you playing?"

He swallows.

"I don't follow you."

"Ever since I stopped being the one chasing you around like a puppy dog."

He looks ahead, distractedly taking an interest in a cat that's disemboweling a sack of garbage. He's trying to get his breath back, to get his ideas back in order. Finally, he turns and faces me again. This time, it's his eyes that don't follow.

"Are you sure you're okay?" he mumbles.

"Positive. Though I'm not sure there's anything positive about it."

"Whoa there! Now you're flirting with paranoia, if you want my opinion."

With outspread hands, I ask him not to get ahead of me.

"Listen, Dine. It's true that I've had a hell of a shock, but from there to suggesting I've lost my marbles as a result, that's not very nice.... First you come over to my home and hustle me out to the fanciest restaurant in town. As if by chance, Madame Rym is at the next table."

"Sheer coincidence."

"Okay, let's pretend it was. Then, this evening you go straight to her house without asking the way."

"I called her earlier in the day to ask for directions."

"You called her?"

"She's not an alien. Her number's in the book."

I nod, completely relaxed.

"So far, so good. Now, let's see if you've got an answer to everything.... Do you expect me to believe you've never set foot in her house before?"

Intrigued, he puts on his puzzled face, as if searching for a flaw in his plans. His eyebrows meet in the middle. Having found nothing compromising, he turns to face me again, not without hostility.

"That's right."

"You've never set foot in her house before this evening?"

His features reveal doubt again, but he gets a grip quickly and thunders, "Never!"

"In that case, how come you know that the library is at the end of the corridor, to the left of the hall, and that there are some fabulous books, a giant TV and a video?"

A tiny detail, insignificant, pointless.... Dine drains of all color. It's as if he's been squeezed dry in an instant. His mouth trembles, unable to frame words, and his Adam's apple hangs suspended in his throat.

With my thumb and index finger, I go "bang" at him and get out of the car.

I don't hear him start up again until I'm on the third-floor landing.

❧

Someone must have paid me a visit while I was at Mme. Rym's. He forgot to turn the lights out. My living room is a shambles: armchairs overturned, lampshades askew and bedcovers torn off. My improvised bookshelf lies on the floor, the books scattered and the drawers tossed aside. Someone has urinated on the curtains in my bedroom and drawn obscene pictures on the walls. A message has been left for me, written in red lipstick and two languages. In Arabic, I am ordered to contact the nearest gravedigger. In French, I am the son of a whore and generally a bad lot.

As I'm assessing the damage, a shadow invades my hallway. I get out my gun and spring into the corridor, finger on the trigger.

"Don't shoot, Uncle Brahim."

It's Fouroulou, a little guy who shares his mother's widowhood on the sixth floor. He puts his hands up, pale and frightened by the size of my weapon.

"You should knock before you come in. I could have killed you."

He nods and lowers his arms.

Fouroulou is our local waif. They say he never sleeps. At the age of seventeen, he's already an embittered old man. Too old for school and too young for a proper job, he's usually up for any kind of hell-raising. He used to come to the house regularly and propose lucrative ventures to my youngest, like dealing in second-hand clothing from Marseilles. A while ago, he started selling bootleg cigarettes. He has a wheelbarrow, which he's converted into a mini-kiosk, on the corner of the street. He's on his stool from dawn to dusk, boom-box blaring, chatting up the girls and giving credit to the city's bums.

I put my gun back in its holster.

"Were you in?"

He ruffles his ginger hair and nods yes.

"What time was it?"

"Dunno."

I go over and lock the door so no one will disturb us, and offer him a chair in the kitchen. He helps himself to a glass of water, swallows it in one gulp and wipes his mouth on his sleeve. He looks harassed. I wait for him to settle down and then ask him:

"How many were there?"

"Four…three of them came in, the other kept watch at the bottom of the stairs."

"Where were you?"

"I was counting my takings on the fifth floor. They came on foot, because I didn't hear a car when they came or when they left.

They didn't wait around on the landing. They had keys. I thought about calling the neighbors, but these guys were armed."

"Can you describe them?"

"They had disguises…."

"Like what?"

"Huge noses, with handlebar moustaches, false eyebrows and berets. One of them took off his wig to scratch his head. But these guys were huge. The smallest of them was well over a hundred kilos. They were here a good ten minutes, and then they left with a shopping bag. They weren't in any hurry."

"Did they say anything?"

"Not really."

"What about their weapons?"

"Shotg—…"

He stops dead, his throat tight, pours himself another glass of water and drains it in one go. The sweat glistens on his temples, trickles down his cheeks and converges on his chin, which is long and pointed, like a funnel.

"I can't identify them, uncle Brahim. I don't know a thing about guns."

"That's okay."

His mottled face flushes. He half stands and says:

"If I had a piece at home, you can bet I'd have drilled some holes in their guts. I was ashamed to sit on my hands while they were chucking everything on the floor. I don't even have a phone, or I'd've called the police."

I clap him on the cheek to show I'm not angry with him.

"You've got nothing to reproach yourself with, son. These guys weren't just petty thieves. They're not scared of police sirens. These were killers. Ruthless shooting machines with no respect for age or sex. They wouldn't have thought twice before smashing your head in if you'd shown yourself. You did right, and I congratulate you. Go back to your mother now, and not a word to anyone."

"I followed them, you know," he adds, as if he couldn't manage to shake off his sense of guilt. "There was a van waiting for them on the other side of the footbridge. A cream-colored Renault J5. I wrote down the number."

※

The crime scene investigators overrun my hideaway early the following morning. I haven't touched anything. To keep out of their way, I retire to the kitchen and do things that don't need doing.

Lino comes back, looking down in the mouth.

He finds my serial setbacks embarrassing and doesn't know what to do. He's afraid of my reaction.

He straddles a chair with his chin resting on the back, and tries to sense my mood.

I feel for his distress. There's no doubt my quarantine has hit him like an amputation.

We've been together for how long? Ten, twelve years? Sorrows? Delights? A whole lifetime wouldn't be long enough to list them. He's become accustomed to my shouting, my lightning-swift changes of heart, my sulks and my manner, that of a frustrated man, not always reasonable, but upright and uncompromising. Yes, I've always automatically played him for my whipping-boy, and held him responsible whenever things get on top of me; yes, I've always considered him small fry and refused to see the merit in him simply because my own has been neglected, but I love him deeply, and he knows it.

The fault line that separated our two generations, and the constant arguments that arose from it, my country-boy upbringing versus his spoon-fed city-boy casualness—all these temperamental and intellectual incompatibilities, far from forcing us apart, have brought us so close together that we are almost indistinguishable. I was always his boss, of course, but I was first and foremost his buddy, his "super," with all the familiarity and intimacy that suggests, and my bad character aroused his affection rather than his irritation.

The stories of some men are like legends in that they contain a basic truth. Ours is so because it is simple. It is the story of a friendship in its raw state, stubborn as love, which demands commitment as well as complicity; a rod of solidarity rolled up in the cloth of tenderness, which automatically unfurls in the sky when the weather gets stormy and cracks loudly in the wind like a sacred banner. I swear the mere sound of it overhead helps you triumph over the worst adversity.

Whenever I catch myself drawing up the inventory of this dog's life of mine, in the deceitful silence of the night, and can't come up with a single scrap of satisfaction; whenever I'm forced to recognize the sheer quantity of my faults and blunders—I, who used to excel in the art of making excuses—that's when I can fall back on this friendship and save the day for myself, for there is no more bitter pill, no more tragic waste, no more pitiable misfortune than to make the maximum number of enemies and not a single friend.

"Do you have any idea who your poltergeists were?"

I make a face.

"I've got a whole heap."

"Maybe they were burglars...."

"Armed to the teeth?"

"That's the fashion, nowadays."

I shake my head. "They weren't thieves."

"So they were trying to do you in."

"They knew I wasn't home."

He nods; it's completely beyond him.

"What did they take?"

"A manuscript I was working on."

"*Magog*?"

"Among other things. My policeman's log too, and two notebooks full of miscellaneous notes, and my family photos, a few newspaper clippings about books...."

"Jewelry?

"Mina took it all with her."

"Cash?"

"Yes, my savings. No big deal. Enough to throw up a smoke-screen, but not to get rich. Did you notice the obscene drawings on the walls?"

"I told the photographer to get some pictures of them. The message isn't signed. Do you think it's an 'emir'?"

"Maybe. I bother people, stir up the shit. It could be anyone: the mafia, politicians, fundamentalists, the people who live off revolution, the guardians of the Temple, even the defenders of the national identity who think the only way to promote the Arabic language is to smash the Frenchifiers. I'm a writer, Lino, the number one *common* enemy."

Lino stands up and paces up and down the room, brow furrowed, pounding his fist silently into the palm of his hand.

He stops in front of the window and watches the street distractedly.

"Goddammit! What kind of country are we living in?"

"That's the wrong question to ask."

A cop comes to tell us that a cream-colored Renault j5 has been found abandoned near the port. I nod him my thanks. He salutes awkwardly and disappears.

"I don't see Ewegh," I say.

"He stayed downstairs."

"Why?"

"How should I know? He's a block of granite. Nobody's managed to work out what he's hiding in there. If you ask me, the way they thanked you shook him up. He doesn't talk about it, but he's been strange ever since he got wind you'd been discharged."

Chapter eight

Hadi Salem has asked me to come and see him in his office. I'm not exactly ecstatic. He's the kind of nut you don't want to meet up with early in the morning if you plan on making anything of your day. But he has the privilege of being very friendly with Sliman Houbel.

His sultanate infests the top floor of a bleak building on the corner of Rue des Trois-Horloges, beside a bustling *souk*. Since the elevator is reserved for the city's VIPs, I climb the one hundred and ten steps to the scaffold without complaint.

A female warder of some kind in a *hijab*, tits the size of airbags, intercepts me in the corridor, checks my papers and hustles me up to the chief of staff. The latter surreptitiously puts something away in his drawer when he sees me arrive. His knife-edge face relaxes when he sees that my ancient suit bears none of the hallmarks of a bigwig. He waves my jailer away with a finger and asks me to sit down in a metal chair suitably placed for passing nobodies.

"You're behind schedule, Mister Llob."

"Just like our country."

He doesn't appreciate my friendly gesture and makes a show of scribbling in a notebook to make me think he's working furiously.

I take out a packet of cigarettes. He immediately points out a sign prohibiting smoking. I accept this and forsake my pollution.

The fellow stops scrawling and leans back to admire his spidery calligraphy. Satisfied, he leans over his notebook and goes back to his absorbing drafting, sticking out his tongue at every capital letter.

Time is beginning to drag, so I take an interest in the furniture. There's a safe in one corner, a worn-out sofa beside a French door with no curtain, a Chinese ashtray on a low table and, on the wall, a dusty canvas depicting a wicker basket filled with lemons—a family portrait, no doubt.

"Does Mister Salem have guests?"

Without raising his head, he points at the wall clock with the tip of his pencil. It is one-thirty.

"He's not here yet?"

His pencil veers to one side and points at a red light shining over the padded door on the left.

"Would you mind enlightening me?"

He puts his pencil down wearily and consents to look at me.

"It is the hour of *dohr**, Mister Llob. Mister Salem is at prayer."

My tactlessness has blocked his inspiration. He reads what he has written, can't get back in his stride, tears out the page, crumples it and tosses it into an astonishingly empty waste-paper basket.

A silence freighted with hostility falls between him and me. After two minutes, he remembers his drawer, takes out a cup of coffee, puts it down in front of him and discovers a juvenile cockroach in his brew. Not even slightly dismayed, he plunges his finger in to rescue the creature and, with a magisterial flick of the wrist, sends it flying across the room.

The lamp switches from red to green.

Unhurriedly, the secretary presses a button and announces me on the intercom.

* *dhor*—second prayer of the day, at 1:30 P.M.

"Show him in!"

Hadi Salem is sitting cross-legged on his prayer mat, like a toad on a blue-green leaf. In his hypocritical way, he wants me to come upon him in the full flow of his asceticism. In my way, I don't understand how he has managed to get to his desk, switch the light to green and answer the intercom without getting up from his prostration.

I have to wait while he finishes his mumbling.

"I'm going to tweak your nose until your ears get pulled into your head," he says, standing up.

And he leaps on me, covering me with extravagant kisses.

"You big pile of shit!" he exults. "Always sticking your nose in where it's not wanted. You irredeemable goddamn pest, you. A straitjacket's too good for you."

He holds me at arm's length to look at me, hugs me to his wrestler's chest and slobbers generously on my cheeks. I feel as if I'm whirling around in the eye of a hurricane.

His warm welcome soon wears him out. With boundless care and attention, he seats me in an armchair and steps back, hands on his hips. *He can't get over it.* He stands there, moved, happy to see that I'm there, before his very eyes, in the flesh—he who used to write the most unflattering reports about me, he who used energetically to encourage my director to break me, he who never hesitated for one second before giving the thumbs-down the moment I was flat on my back with my legs in the air.

"You crazy low-down bastard sonofabitch! You've no idea how happy I am to see you again. It's been ages, hasn't it?"

Salem and I graduated in the same year. We did the same Intelligence Officer's training course in '63. He failed every module and was transferred into administration. He looked after the army's welfare fund for years, building palaces in every town, as many for himself as for his clients. He certainly caught on fast. The country was divided into two franchises. On the one hand, the land of the smooth operators, the ass-kissers and horse-traders; on the other, that of the chosen people, the killjoys and baby-eaters. He made his choice and he's not complaining. While I was hunting delinquents, he was sailing in a choppy sea. Having no particular specialty—which would just be a source of hassles anyway—he developed something of a skill in corruption and the forging of invoices. Result: he's rich as Croesus, with control of an influential division at a ministerial level, and people respond to his asinine utterances as if they were infallible prophecies.

He perches a buttock on the edge of his desk, crosses his fingers over one knee and goes on admiring me.

"Good old pig-headed Brahim! The things we have to do to put his head on a spike! You haven't changed one iota, you bastard. Do you remember when we were going through retraining at the academy, at Soumaa? Come to think of it, what happened to that housekeeper we used to argue over all day? What was her name? Wardia? Remember the chassis on her? Sonofabitch! I could never save a cent, with her around."

He lets loose a gigantic laugh and goes on, "And Sergeant Kada? God! How you drove him up the wall! You nearly drove him to the loony-bin... (his voice goes down suddenly). You were a hoot in those days, Brahim. You were something else. What got into you that you've turned a hundred and eighty degrees?"

"It's down to the wind, Hadi, the wind."

"The wind changes, and so do weathercocks."

"Not the wind of speechifiers and rabble-rousers."

His hands separate and slide up his thigh. He becomes somber.

"We're friends, Brahim, right?"

"If you say so."

"I do say so. My eyes are clear. I can see beyond your empty, embarrassing ranting. I see like a man who is informed, who knows where he came from and where he's going, what he wants and what he has to hand over to others, what he can and what he can't do. You, on the other hand, you just hurl yourself into the abyss, blinkered by your own reckless stupidity.... What's happening to you pains me. It has to be said you deserve it, but I'd be sorry if the police ended up losing a valuable asset like you. It would be a waste, Brahim, a terrible waste."

"...."

"Three days ago I had a conversation with Sliman Houbel. He flew off the handle when I mentioned you. I swear to God, I think you went too far with your shitty little book. It's extraordinarily cavalier. I don't say you don't have talent. On the contrary, your pen is worth its weight in gold...."

"And how much does a pen weigh?"

"Let's stick to the subject, shall we? I'm trying to clean up the mess you've made. Try not to show your ingratitude. It took me two godawful hours to convince Sliman. It would have taken less time to convince a *mullah*, and you know it. Last I heard, the letter announcing your retirement had been withdrawn. At the request of the Minister. We took an insane risk. Don't disappoint us."

Seeing that I'm not too impressed, he goes on, "With a bit of luck, you'll be back in your job before the end of the month. Your men are demoralized. Your lieutenant has put in for a transfer. I sent a superintendent down to Headquarters. It's like a nursing home down there these days. Your director even requested a meeting to have you reinstated."

I ask permission to smoke.

He grants it.

"I'm genuinely moved," I say, blowing smoke in his direction. "On the other hand, I must deserve it."

He goes behind his desk. The moment of truth. He joins his hands delicately under his chin and focuses his "clear" eyes on me. A grave silence follows, vitiated slightly by the distant sounds of the *souk*.

"Before you answer me, take some time to think. I know you, you're impulsive and touchy, and I'd prefer to wait a week if that's what it takes. For heaven's sake, Brahim, don't say anything right away. Just listen, then go home and think."

"I'm ready."

He breathes deeply and wipes himself nervously with a handkerchief. It's as if his career, his fortune, his fate depend on my decision.

"You must admit publicly that you were misguided, that your book is an unfortunate initiative, the product of a difficult time...."

Don't say anything, I beg you. It's not the end of the world, after all. We're not asking the impossible. A short announcement in the press, without a lot of fuss. If you like, you can go on television. Noureddin Boudali has agreed to have you on his show. He's the best. He'll set it up any way you want. Two words, Brahim, two pitiful little words: *I regret....*"

This time, the silence is absolute. You can hear the blood rushing through Hadi's temples. Even the echoes of the *souk* have died down. Hadi Salem is drowning in sweat.

I stub out my cigarette in the ashtray and stand up. Hadi Salem is hanging on my words, imploring.

I say, "The only thing I regret is coming here to see you."

He trembles. His anxiety turns instantly to anger. His pupils, previously glassy, are inflamed with inexpressible hatred. He braces himself against his desk, then leans back in his chair and considers me intently.

"My conscience will be clear, at least," he says.

I don't need a diagram to understand what he means.

⁊⋆

It's a red car with tinted windows. It has a long scratch down the left wing. I think I saw it this morning, parked opposite the garage where I went to pick up my own rattletrap. There was someone inside, because a shadow moved. I didn't pay much attention. And there it is again, on the corner of Rue des Trois-Horloges, two wheels up on the curb and two in the gutter.

I go into the first café I find.

"Do you have a telephone?" I ask.

"There's a post office in the square," the owner retorts. He's in front of me, frantically polishing the counter. "Are you ill?"

"Not really."

He looks at me askance.

"You're pale and your hands are shaking."

"A chill, maybe."

"In this heat?"

He's on his guard.

It's not surprising, given the spate of home-made bombs people hide in any old container and leave on counters.

A hulk appears, framed in the doorway. Built like a bouncer, he drowns the room in shadow. Sheltering behind sunglasses, he turns his head from left to right, pauses on me and then leaves, releasing a dazzling wave of light.

"What can I get you?"

"A mineral water."

I quench my thirst under the more and more intrigued gaze of the owner, pay and make myself scarce.

Outside, the street is swarming with people, but the red car has vanished.

It catches up with me two days later, on the Boulevard Mohammed v. Just as I decide to get to the bottom of this business, it leaves at top speed and disappears round the first corner.

The little circus lasts the rest of the week. They obviously mean to be indiscreet. A red car, always the same one, parked so as to attract attention…. They're trying to put the frighteners on me. They would have gone about it a different way if they had wanted to eliminate me.

On the eighth day, there it is, frolicking about in my rear-view mirror again. This time it's too much. I head for a suburban housing development, leave my car in a courtyard, plunge into one of the buildings, cross the terrace and come out through an emergency exit on the other side. I skirt round two blocks and come at them from behind.

The red car is lurking in a deserted alleyway, two hundred meters from mine. I approach it on tiptoe, hugging the walls, my hand in my jacket.

"Nobody move!" I shout, nearly tearing the door off, my gun fearless.

The man doesn't move.

He's slumped against the steering wheel, arms dangling and eyes bulging.

Somebody got there ahead of me and wrung his neck.

༒

That evening, troubled by the way things are going, I come upon a young man on my landing. He's dirty and disheveled, his faunlike features spiky with the beard of a convict. I've never seen him in the area before. Without waiting to ask questions, I pounce on him like a madman and clout him on the temple with my nine-millimeter.

"Uncle Brahim," yells Fouroulou, swarming up the stairs at maximum speed. "He's my cousin. He's a bit simple."

I reckon he's not the only one.

I let him go and run to take refuge in my dump of a home.

Chapter nine

I've been watching the crowd of sleepwalkers circling around in front of the Grande Poste through the window of a tea-room for an hour, and I haven't spotted one familiar face. People come and go in a frantic ebb and flow, not even noticing when they collide with each other. Their shipwrecked gaze sees not even a speck of land. They don't seem even slightly put out by the danger awaiting them just around the corner. Last week, a car bomb went off about a hundred meters from here. The mangled bodies had to be gathered up with teaspoons. As soon as the sirens of the fire engines died down, life picked up again as if nothing had happened. Death, once it has become banal, is just part of the furniture. It's the calm afterwards that seems suspicious.

Opposite me, a heavily made-up woman is making eyes at me. She's holding onto her glass of lemonade as if it were life itself, yet the lines on her face tell no lies. This woman is lonely: she's looking for a friend. She's noticed my solitude, and that's why she feels we're alike.

"Do you have a cigarette?"

Without waiting for me to reach for my pocket, she leaves her table and sits down at mine, her glass in her fist like a trophy.

"I'm waiting for someone," I warn her.

"We're all waiting for someone, but we don't know who it is."

She helps herself to a cigarette from the pack I hold out and rolls it distractedly between her scrawny fingers. Her smile is sad.

"I've been watching you for quite a while," she confesses.

"To tell the truth, I noticed right away."

"You must think I'm trying to pick you up."

"That would be very flattering."

She fumbles about in her cheap handbag, gets out a disposable lighter, lights her cigarette and turns away to blow out the smoke.

"I'm not a whore."

"I didn't say anything."

"But you're thinking it…. I look like one, but I'm not a hooker, Mister Llob. I have a profession that's a bit like a vice. You smoke, you sleep around sometimes, but you never solicit."

"Do I know you?"

She waves her hand casually.

"We've met…."

She examines the reddish tip of her cigarette intently.

"We even worked together for a whole weekend."

"Are you a cop?"

"In a way, but not really: I'm a journalist … well, I used to be."

I try to find something I remember in her ravaged features, looking deep into her eyes. I can't find a trace of her in my memory banks.

"Malika," she prompts, irritated by my lapse.

It doesn't help. I catalogue her faded dress, crudely patched at the shoulder, the criss-crossed cheeks, the mouth that evidently doesn't laugh very often, the wild hair, which lends her a demonic air, the odor of wretchedness oozing from her pores….

"The bank thing in '78," she sighs. "The two stiffs in the vault."

I clap my hand to my forehead.

"Malika Sobhi! How could I forget?"

"How can anyone remember, the mess we're in nowadays, everything turned upside down? Still, it was a long time ago. Those were revolutionary times, chasing sorcerers and reactionaries.... And yet I remembered you just like that," she says, snapping her fingers. "True, you've put on weight and gone a bit grey at the temples, but you've kept the essentials."

"I must admit I can't say the same...."

"It's different for me. My own mother would have to look twice. Sickness has left its mark on me (she taps her head). Two fits of depression, two years in the freak ward. I used to go out on the street stark naked. It was hard, very hard.... I lost my husband in a bombing and the best part of my reason in the Association for the Victims of Terrorism, where I'm still active."

"I'm sorry to hear it."

"You're just about the only one, let me tell you. If you only knew how people treat us. I even got beaten up," she adds, letting her hair drop down on my arm to show me a scar on her scalp. "They said I was an agitator, Mister Llob. They tried to beat it into my skull with clubs."

A waiter in a tie comes over, apologizes to me politely, takes the woman firmly by the arm and says, "You're bothering the gentleman. Go back to your table, please."

"Did anyone call you?" I ask, outraged.

Flustered, he gulps convulsively and explains, "This woman harasses our customers, sir."

"I pay my way," Malika protests.

"We don't want your money, madam. This is a tea-room, not a night-club."

I ask him to let it drop. He looks the woman up and down, with disgust in his eyes, nods and retreats, backwards.

"Bastard," Malika mutters. "He thinks I'm round the bend. He doesn't realize that any of us can hit rock bottom in this country, from one day to the next."

I take her hands in mine to comfort her.

"Is there anything I can do for you?"

I hadn't planned to, but I have touched a raw nerve. Her eyes open wide, horrified. She shudders from head to foot. Her bony cheeks become more so.

"What? What did you say?"

She pushes my hands away and stands up dramatically.

"I don't need your idiotic pity, Mister Llob. I just needed to talk to someone."

"Don't get me wrong, I beg you. I didn't mean any offense."

"You're all the same!"

"...Malika, listen to me...."

"Hands off, you filthy copper!"

Everyone in the room freezes and watches us. Malika Sobhi is reduced to a disheveled wreck, frothing at the mouth and wild-eyed. She flings her cigarette in my face, gathers up her handbag and runs away.

I try to catch her.

She rushes into the crowd and disappears without turning round.

"I told you she was nuts," the waiter whispers in my ear, happy to have the last word.

＊

I've come to watch the sea having it out with the rocks of the shore, beneath the mewing of the gulls as they hover about in the spray. The hysterical waves have forced the fishermen to beat a retreat toward the old jetty. The beach is completely submerged and the roar of the bay is distressing. I've been standing here for I don't know how long, and now I'm wandering about for a bit, at the whim of my resentments.

I don't see the sun call it a day, nor do I see the evening brooding as night approaches. I don't even know how I've ended up in front of Sid Ali's joint.

Sid Ali is solemnly waving a fan over his grill. To keep himself going, he's breathing in the smoke of the fire and licking his lips. When he sees me on the threshold, he pauses, puts down the fan and wipes his chubby hands on an apron that's zebra-striped with gravy.

"You're still among the living!" he exclaims, rolling toward me like a wave.

I receive him full in the face and crumple under the weight of his affection. His crematorium smell is suffocating.

"Are you upset with me? We never see you."

"It's better that way."

He raises his eyebrows.

"Why are you talking such rubbish?"

"My mouth is obviously depressed."

"What's the worst that could happen? Friends aren't just for the good times."

"My father taught me to share my happiness and keep my suffering to myself."

"He was wrong."

He steps back and sizes me up, then digs a finger into my gut.

"You look like somebody's knocked the stuffing out of you," he asserts, offering me a chair. "Are you passing through or do you want to eat?"

"Both."

"I close in less than an hour. How would you like to eat at my house? The kids would love to see you again."

"Don't press me. I don't feel well. And it won't be long before Lino turns up here. Fix me up half a dozen *merguez* with butter and a whole lot of mustard, and put it on my tab because I'm broke."

He goes off to wait on two customers at the end of the room and then comes back.

"Where have you been?"

"Don't you know?"

He pulls a face.

"No."

"They took away my badge."

He avoids my eye for a moment, scratching the top of his skull, then crams himself into the chair next to me.

"Ah! ..."

"You don't seem surprised."

He waves his hand vaguely.

"I own a restaurant, and I don't have much of an education, but that doesn't mean I've got a dick on my shoulders. After all, what's a war on the fundamentalists worth if it doesn't start a war against honest citizens too? You're neither the first nor the last. Frankly, I don't want to talk about it. I've puked up so often these last few years that I don't bother with the other end any more. Besides, what did you expect at your age? That they'd take away your trousers into the bargain?"

Dropping the nonchalant tone, he digs his elbow into my side. "Go on, give us a smile. Have you heard the latest? What do you call a kangaroo that won't come back?"

"If you mean a boomerang, the answer's a coat hanger, and you're a prize asshole."

He throws his head back and laughs the laugh of a fat man, setting the rolls of his belly quivering.

"Have you heard it before?"

Ten minutes later, he's putting a chipped plate down in front of me, loaded with kebabs, sliced onions, green peppers and bread; and there's a big jug filled with an absolutely revolting house concoction. He settles down opposite me, his face resting between his hands, and watches me stuff myself.

"What's the plan?"

"Beat the jinx."

"Don't make such a fuss, please. It's not the end of the world. There's more to life than being a cop. Haven't you had enough, after all these years? Do me a favor: put it behind you. There's no point being a Don Quixote. That's the way the world is. The Messiah himself couldn't fix it. Truth is, when he comes back he'll blow it to bits once and for all. It's not that I don't understand you. You're burying your head in the sand. You're not the poor man's lawyer, still less the lawman sent from heaven. You're just a two-bit functionary. You do your work; you go to bed, full stop, the end. I'm not saying you shouldn't give a damn, that you shouldn't lift your little finger. I'm just saying you don't have to try to fart higher than your ass. The important thing is not to cheat. Have you been cheating? You haven't been cheating. If other people have, it's not down to you. Tomorrow, up there, everyone will have to face his own conscience."

"For heaven's sake, Sid Ali, can't you see I'm eating?"

"So now you eat with your ears? Hey, how do you expect me to stop yakking if you won't say a word?"

ᴪ

Lino has cut off his ponytail. He's liberated his temples and tidied up his forelock. On the other hand, he hasn't shaved since the last time we saw each other. His flowery tropical shirt, his jeans with the knees showing through and his bootleg trainers make him look like some juvenile delinquent fresh from the sticks.

He greets Sid Ali with a casual wave of his finger and signals to me to join him.

Behind him, Ewegh Seddig is keeping a lookout on the street. His colossal bulk almost eclipses their car. Planted solidly on his heels, arms folded across his chest, he dominates the sidewalk, as impenetrable as his dark glasses. I once asked him why he wore glasses at night that were supposed to protect against sunlight. He replied, with disdain, that it was to protect everyone else against his eyes.

I wipe my mouth and hands with a cloth and hurry over to my place in the car. Lino takes the wheel. Ewegh checks the surrounding area before taking over the back seat.

"How are you doing?" I ask.

"Hmm...."

Lino drives us to the other side of Bab El-Oued, goes into Place Premier Mai and races along the sea front. He says nothing, one hand on the steering wheel and the other arm resting on the sill. Every now and again, to break the silence, he pretends to take an interest in a passer-by, watching him in the rear view mirror for a while and then forgetting him a few meters further on.

Lino's not himself.

We arrive at a brightly lit tea-room near Maquam. At the bottom of the hill, Algiers is mobilizing her lights to dissuade the shadows from taking up residence in people's minds.

We take a table in a corner, so that we can keep an eye on the room and on our car in the parking lot. A neat young waiter comes over to take our order. Lino orders three orange juices and three chocolate croissants for us.

"How about stopping your little charade now?" I suggest, exasperated.

Lino keeps us in suspense. He breathes on his glasses, wipes them on his shirt and shoves them back onto his eyebrows.

"I'm not well."

"Nor am I."

The waiter comes back with a tray and gives us our food, visibly impressed by the Touareg's bulk. Lino reassures him, "He doesn't bite."

The waiter shakes his head and leaves without claiming a tip.

In a tone of disgust, Lino announces, "We've ID'd the guy who was following you... his name was Farhat Nabilou."

"Is it his name that's got you in such a state?"

"It's his file. Empty as a politician's speech. I was hoping for a bit of detail to find out where he sprang from. Nothing. Farhat Nabilou, born 2 February 1965 in Algiers. Dealer in second-hand goods in El Harrach. No political activity. No convictions. No known associates. A complete loner. Goodnight, end of story. His neighbors don't know much about him. He used to shut up shop at the same time every night and go home straight afterwards."

"He was carrying a gun...."

"That's the thing. The gun belonged to a sergeant who was murdered two years ago in Sidi Moussa. The lab guys are positive. It's the same weapon that blew away three citizens in Rouiba at the beginning of the month."

"Why?"

"They got tired of being pushed around."

"Have you been to Rouiba?"

"With Ewegh, yesterday and this morning. We went door to door, and no one recognized Nabilou from the picture."

"What about the car?"

"Stolen in Chlef, three weeks ago. Souped up, spray job, fake plates, fake registration, borrowed hubcaps and bumpers…. Quite a number, for a solid citizen."

He gulps down half his juice and half his pastry and adds, "Must be a new recruit."

"Was he a follower?"

"Nobody saw him at the mosque. But that doesn't mean anything. When there's a war on, you'll take anyone."

"Was he married?"

"Divorced, no children. His mother's dead. His father's an invalid. It's a dead end, really it is."

I rotate my glass in my hands pensively.

Ewegh hasn't touched his. He's watching the outside, stiff as a cobra on the scent.

"Who broke his neck?" I throw into the mixture. "To my knowledge at least, there haven't been any traveling circuses since '62. So where did he come from, this Hercules?"

Ewegh doesn't move a muscle.

Lino, for his part, seems bored.

"I didn't even have time to go round the buildings," I continue. "That took me five, six minutes. And I find him slumped over the steering wheel. Can you explain it, lieutenant?"

"He was being followed too, that must be it."

My finger settles unerringly on the Touareg.

"It was you…."

"His neck snapped in my hand," Ewegh admits immediately, as if we were talking about a minor accident. "I was just trying to get him out of his car."

Lino sighs. He confesses, "The boss got Ewegh to watch you. After the thing with the poltergeists, we got a phone call at HQ. An anonymous call. The guy said they were after your hide. It might have been a hoax, but the boss preferred to take it at face value. Ewegh was detailed to protect you from a distance. The other day, it's true, he wanted to arrest the guy. You're right: alive, he might have been able to clear some things up…. It was an accident."

Ewegh doesn't demur.

He's watching the parking lot and ignoring everything else.

Lino's tone changes abruptly:

"You want to do me a favor, Super? Join Mina and the kids in Bejaya, go back to Igidher, lose yourself in Oran, but don't hang around here. I'm not happy about it at all. Nobody's happy...."

I'm about to tell him what I really think of his advice when, *Boom*! the plate-glass window shatters into a million pieces. A whirlwind picks me up and catapults me backwards. I hear screaming around me. I have trouble understanding what's happened. I'm groggy, and I can't even lift the table that's overturned on top of me. Lino is stretched out beside me, eyes staring. All four limbs flailing, Ewegh is trying to free himself of the chairs piled up all over him.

The tea-room has been turned upside down. The people who had been sitting by the entrance are buried under rubble. I recognize the waiter among the shattered rag dolls. He is just realizing, horrorstruck, that his arm has gone missing. Incredulous and furious, he won't admit it to himself. A woman is reeling about in the dust cloud, her hands outstretched like a monster escaped from a horror movie, her face removed in the explosion.

"Where's my bag?" cries a young girl, covered in blood, as she searches frantically in the dust.

She doesn't seem to notice the mutilated man under her nose, nor the disembodied leg bleeding all over her calf.

"It's a bomb! It's a bomb!" someone calls out in delirium.

Ewegh is the first to get up, in an avalanche of dust. He puts to one side the table that has been crushing me and picks me up.

"Are you okay?"

Apart from a few splinters of glass in my arm, I don't think I'm injured.

Lino groans. His foot is horribly twisted.

"My ankle hurts," he says, gasping.

A man with a blackened face appears through the smoke, stumbles and collapses, his back carbonized. A miraculously unharmed woman sits on a chair looking around in all directions. She can't comprehend it. A flame leaps up behind the counter, sending its reptilian tongue into a curtain and spreading rapidly toward the ceiling. The roof cracks, tears open and collapses with a crash.

Outside, there is total chaos.

Shadows move about, blend into each other and run around as if in a hallucinatory vision. Their clamoring rises to an insane, deafening torrent of sound.

"Where's my son?" a ragged father beseeches people on bended knee. "He was there, right there. Where is he? …"

"It's not true, it's not true, it's not true!" an old man repeats, shaking his head in denial. "It's not true, it's not true…."

The fire sneaks into the parking lot, engulfs a car and starts blowing up the remainder in a surreal cacophony of noise. Human torches disappear into the blackness, like fireflies, their movements more distressing than their screams. Within a few minutes, the Belvedere has been transformed into a nightmare, and hell seems less forbidding than this purgatory.

Part III

On a blade of grass
he tries in vain to rest,
the heavy dragonfly

Matsuo Basho, *The Wandering Monk*
(1644–1694)

Chapter ten

Dying is the worst offence you can do to your friends.

Da Achour is no more.

He ate like four men and smoked his usual cigarette between eight-thirty and eight-thirty precisely; and then, comfortably ensconced in his rocking chair, he put his feet up on the balustrade, gave a gentle kick to start the chair rocking and, while gazing at the lights of a cruise ship in the offing, he surreptitiously departed this life in the middle of a weary belch.

If I had been in the neighborhood, I'm sure I would have seen our merciful God among the stars, congratulating himself upon receiving him among His own.

In a way, he was family. In his eyes lay a whole market in twilit images of nostalgia. He was a haven of wisdom, my piece of Igidher and the lost years. God got a bargain; as for me, I'm bereft.

Already the sea is lamenting, already the silence is shrinking back, and already the world is *empty*.

Da Achour was one of the Just.

I will miss him greatly.

He used to say: "Race isn't a question of white, black, red or yellow. Men can't appreciate nature's talents. They make prejudices out of differences; they call it segregation. Race isn't a question of Arabs, Jews, Slavs or Tutsis. Men don't know how to take advice from Time. They're content to dragoon people into ethnic groups. By creating a hierarchy of humanity they hope to compensate for their own insignificance and avenge their own vulgarity.... Race? True race? There are only two: the Noble Race and the Ignoble Race; Good People and Odious People. They've been at each other's throats since the dawn of time. Such is the balance of things. They were there before the Light and before the prophets, and they'll survive all civilizations. We've been taught to hate ever since we came into the world; we were turned away from the Truth. We're taught hatred of the Other, hatred of the Absent and the Foreign—a manufactured hatred, in short. And look, Brahim, just look. Who's burning our schools today, who's killing our brothers and neighbors, who's beheading our intellectuals, who's putting our land to fire and the sword? Aliens? Malaysians? Animists? Christians? ... They're Algerians, just Algerians, who not so long ago were belting out the national anthem in our stadiums, who rushed in their thousands to help the victims of disasters and mobilized impressively for every telethon. And now look. Do you recognize yourself in them?—I don't, not at all.... *My* race of people, Brahim, are all those who, from one end of the world to the other, refuse to allow these monsters to be forgiven."

He was my mausoleum, the last patron saint of the city.

⅔

We bury him in the cemetery at Igidher. Fifty graves beyond Idir Naït-Wali. Recently dug graves, still fresh, that scar the earth with brownish bruises. Drama has struck the tribe twice in between times. First, a band of fundamentalists set up a fake road block on the road to Sidi Lakhdar. They opened fire on a bus without warning. The vehicle caught fire, burning the passengers alive. The screams of the victims still resonate in the silence of the night. Then they abducted seven women and thirteen children from the shrine at Sidi Mezian. They were found in a field two days later, with their throats slit.

Mohand asks me if I have anything to say in memory of the deceased.

I shake my head.

"Okay, there are cars to take you to Imazighen. We'll meet up there in an hour or so."

I thank him. And he goes back to his armed men.

The crowd disperses in silence. The old men hobble toward their vans or carts. The younger ones begin to climb down the steep slope of the hill toward Imazighen.

Arezki Naït-Wali is on a large rock in front of Da Achour's grave, lost in thought. His sweat-stained shirt is steaming in the heat. He's waiting for me to come for him, with his crimson nose hidden behind a kerchief.

"Come on," I say, "let's go."

His chin quivers. He stands up.

I put my arm around his shoulders and push him ahead of me.

"Shall we go by car?"

"I'd rather walk."

"It's not exactly next door," I warn him.

"It's not bad once you get down the hill."

"Okay, it's a deal. Let's walk."

۴

Imazighen is a ghostly village a few hundred meters from Igidher. In the good old days, this was where they parked members of the tribe stubborn enough to refuse to join the *Zouaves*.* During the war, it came under SAS† control. After '62, it chose to remain a place of exclusion, and it has reveled in its rejected-outcast pathology ever since. Not a weeping child, not a clattering saucepan. There it is, modestly

---

* *Zouave*: corps of French infantry first raised in Algeria in 1831 and recruited solely from the Zouaves, a tribe of Berbers (Kabyls) from the mountains of the Jurjura range.

† SAS: *Section administrative spécialisée* (Special Administrative Section), created by the French army in 1955 to establish contact with the Muslim population and weaken nationalist influence in rural areas.

concealing its poverty at the end of a path, behind ramparts of cacti, as depressing as an Indian cemetery. Its people left the day after a massacre, abandoning their scrawny livestock and the tools of their trade to the fundamentalists. Most of the hovels have lost their roofs. The facades, at the mercy of the wind, are crazed and peeling. The wind eddies around in the silence, causing doors to slam and windows to creak. Rats have created kingdoms for themselves amid the decay. And spiders stretch their hanging gardens from one wall to another, high above the furniture. Apart from a few old men haunting their porches like ghosts, only a handful of families have remained obstinately on their land, guns on their shoulders and eyes ever fearful.

"We told them they could come back to Igidher, but they won't leave their vegetable gardens," a young patriot explains to me. "During the day, they do what they can, and at night they keep watch."

"If they carry on like that, they'll be killed by fear and insomnia, if that red trash doesn't get them first."

The young patriot fingers his Kalashnikov and explains, "We patrol the area from time to time. But sometimes a search can take several days, and we're short of men."

I stop to take the measure of the devastation. Abused, traumatized, mistrustful, Imazighen personifies sacrifice. Its alleyways are infected with a new disease: hostility. The hostility of a baffled population, which, nerves raw, refuses to believe that it is possible to be defeated by oversight.

When I was a child, I used to come here often to spy on Lounja. She lived in a small house, now ruined, over there on the hillock behind the cactus. Clad in a loincloth with all the colors of summer, she would go down the path to the spring every day, a jar balanced atop her flaming hair.

Lounja was eleven years old. Her eyes were pale blue. When her crystal-clear laughter rang out through the air, strange frissons would go up and down my spine.

The *imam* wipes himself with a piece of his turban. His scarlet face is about to explode. He leans over Arezki and tells a story: "In '94, forty of those sons of dogs came out of the woods over there. Within an hour they had looted everything. Before they left, they gathered all the families together in the square and preached them a sermon. Then, to set an example, they slit the *muezzin*'s throat, and his son's, and hung them both up by their feet at the entrance to the mosque. You must remember Haj Boudjema, Arezki. He used to teach in the Koranic school at Igidher during the occupation."

"I don't remember him."

"He was a good friend of your father's."

"I don't remember him either."

"Maybe, you were too young.... In '95, they came back. The day before *eid*, can you believe it? They set fire to the homes of former *mujaheddin* and burned Amran and his family to death in the clinic. Surely you remember Amran, the horse dealer?"

Arezki grimaces evasively.

The *imam* frowns, "You don't remember Amran?"

"Sorry."

"I hope you remember me, at least."

Arezki looks down at the ground, "I was very young when I left here."

The *imam* is disappointed.

"Why did they burn him to death?" I ask.

The *imam* turns his palms up to heaven.

"Who knows? Amran was an ordinary person, nobody special. My guess is that they wanted him to handle some stolen livestock in the *souk* and he refused."

We reach the house of old Taos. She welcomes us in the courtyard of her shack, where some rugs and worn-out cushions have been spread out, and asks us to sit down at some low tables arranged around a carob tree.

"Lalla," murmurs the *imam*, looking greedily at the spread, "we're ashamed to make you even poorer."

"My dear *imam*," she breaks in, "you have enough trouble persuading me on Fridays, so I don't think you're going to pull the wool over my eyes today, under my own roof."

The *imam* laughs heartily and goes off to fight for a place among the old men.

Lalla Taos is Da Achour's older sister. The years don't seem to weigh on her at all. She's all of eighty-six, but she's still on the ball, steady and lucid, her movements lively and her responses lightning swift, sometimes marvelously spiced with mischievous details. She is funny and spontaneous, authoritarian without being a tyrant, and she is held in veneration by one and all. Like a spreading oak tree, she has remained upright during the torment; her soul will never be touched by the deep grooves conspiring to disfigure her face, and nor will it be worn down by worry or persecution. She has survived the chaos of the century with rare dignity, the ravages of epidemics and the loss of those close to her, and seems to go through the vicissitudes of life as easily as a needle through cloth. All by herself, she embodies the silent, timeless strength of her people.

I kiss the top of her head.

She wraps her stringy arms around me, then steps back to look at me.

"What are you going to do without your old friend, Brahim?" She feels more sorrow for me than for the deceased.

She's the one who brought me up. I was the apple of her eye. When I got up to mischief it cheered her up; when I was down, she was distressed. She loved me so much that she didn't hesitate to go up the steep hill twice a day to tell my mother to leave me alone.

"He was a saint," I say.

"I'm not worried about him. He was a righteous man. I'm sure he's already on his way to an easy life up there. True, he did behave like a complete delinquent sometimes, but boys like him don't have much to reproach themselves with. The good Lord will give him a slap on the wrist, so no one gets envious, and leave him alone for the rest of eternity…. Right now I'm more worried about you."

"Well, give me a slap on the wrist and say no more about it."

The guests spread out among the tables and immediately start nibbling at the heaps of couscous.

"Come with me," she whispers. "I'll show you something."

She takes me by the hand and leads me into a crumbling room.

"Let's agree on one thing right away," she says. "*They* won't get away with it."

"You have my word."

My word isn't enough for her. She interlaces her fingers with mine and twists our hands around in a childlike oath—like the old days. Reassured, she fumbles about at the back of an ancient sideboard, digs out a padlocked leather chest and opens it in front of me.

"What's this?" she says exultantly, showing me a catapult.

"My *astak*!"

"That's right. I made it for you myself. God, you were so envious of the other kids. And this? Do you remember this?" she says, showing me a small leather pouch sewn shut on all four sides. "This is the charm you used to wear on your arm. It protected you from the evil eye and from evil companions.... And this? You'll never guess. This was going to be your very first fez, but you never wore it. I was taken in by that traveling merchant, curse him. I had never seen a bra before. I thought it was a pair of skullcaps and I asked him to cut one off for you. Achour nearly split his sides laughing when I showed it to him."

To see her still laughing at this fifty-year-old anecdote, pulling out fragments of my childhood one by one as if they were holy relics, leafing through our shared stories as if they were a book of fairy tales, rejoicing in such simple, innocent memories ... what a feeling!

Finally, with infinite care and attention, she gets out what she must consider the centerpiece of her collection and hides it behind her back, her eyes shining.... "Guess, guess what I've got here, big man." I examine her eyes, which have awakened out of their dullness, the flourishing tattoos on her face, her desiccated shoulders shaking with excitement....

"*Do you remember?*"

And she holds out a yellowing, almost washed out photograph....

"*Do you remember?*"

In the photo, it's *her*, eyes screwed up into the sun, sitting astride a donkey, robe pulled up to her knees, radiant, utterly content, totally entranced by the laughing little ragamuffin standing on a fallen tree trunk beside her.

"God, I was ugly."

"You weren't ugly, Brahim. In fact, you were quite good-look-ing."

She strokes my grizzled cheeks and puts her head to one side tenderly, maternally, emotionally: "You were the best."

Chapter eleven

Mohand is insistent that no one must go beyond the grayish ridge that divides the mountain in two like a butcher's cleaver. Fundamentalists sometimes appear among the thickets, watching the village or kidnapping an isolated shepherd. Before, they would go so far as to shoot at anything within range of their guns, and then vanish into the forest. They used this trick to suck patriots into devastating ambushes. Now that their ruses don't work any more, they content themselves with spying on people and attacking the unwise, often children straggling home.

While Arezki and I have been wandering at memory's whim, two guardian angels have been following us at a distance since morning. I spotted them from the start, and I've been acting unsuspecting to keep them on their toes.

We climb a misshapen outcrop that crumbles beneath our feet. The dry grass scratches at our ankles. Arezki is struggling valiantly not to fall behind, but in vain. He has to stop every hundred meters to get his breath back.

"Some cure," he pants.

"It's hard work, but it's good for you."

"Give me a hand, will you?"

I hold out my stick and haul him up to where I am.

"Just a bit more. The view's worth the effort."

He collapses at my feet, his face distorted and his throat parched.

"Pass me your flask. I'm burning up inside."

I sit down beside him.

On our left is the orchard where we used to come for plunder as young tearaways. Now, it's just a shadow of its former, mythical, self. Its silence is fatal. Its sparrows have deserted it. In those days, when its almond trees were in bloom, the hillside was covered in snow all the way to the horizon. Today, not even donkeys dare to enter it.

Arezki, too, is looking at what remains of the orchard of our memories: withered, twisted trees, their branches raised heavenward in desperate prayer.

"Do you remember the day you took a tumble over there, with the watchman right on your tail?"

Arezki shivers and hugs his knees.

"Most of the time he turned a blind eye. He never bothered me."

"That was just to entice his little lambs, make them trust him. I think the wind pressing your *gandoura** against your plump little bottom must have given him ideas."

Arezki shakes his head, a mite irritated. He was always a bit of a prude. Coarse language makes him uncomfortable.

"Do you know why your stories smell bad, Brahim?"

"Because my wit is next door to my ass."

"Spot on."

I laugh.

"I never did see a hare take off as fast as you did."

"Hey!…"

Arezki picks up a twig and snaps it between his fingers. His mouth relishes the undoing of an enigmatic smile.

* *Gandoura*: robe

I lift up a clod of earth with my stick, frightening a swarm of tiny creatures.

At the foot of the outcrop, the river opens up the guts of the earth, its pebbles like fossilized entrails. Once upon a time, swarms of women used to come here to do their washing. The water cascaded down the mountainside and meandered across the distant plain. The reeds jostled each other along its banks, trying to impress the oleanders. The riverbed was deep in some places. We used to splash about to our heart's content, surrounded by an artist's palette of forest noises and dazzling splashes of color. Sometimes, we would pretend to drown and watch our puppies whimper and leap about on the banks until they joined in with spectacular dives. For my part, I didn't swim much. I preferred to hide in the reeds and spend hours watching Lounja. The water would be up to her knees, her hair like a river of gold down her back; her wet robe would reveal her budding breasts, lovely as a pair of flaming suns.

"This is where I painted my very first canvas," Arezki says. "With bits of colored chalk dipped in milk. My mother nearly strangled me when she saw what I'd done to the only sheet she had."

"You were already a genius."

A tractor appears, boastfully climbing the dusty road. It jolts about comically in the ruts, disappears behind a thicket and reappears at the foot of the outcrop. The mayor thanks the driver and jumps to the ground, his rifle slung over his shoulder like a bandolier. The machine coughs as it describes a half-circle and moves off again in an ungainly fashion.

"You two are a pair in a million," says the mayor.

He climbs the hillside nimbly, despite his sixty-odd years, and comes over to sit opposite us.

Akli Uld Ameur was an entrepreneur in the construction industry before the arrival of the "Caliphs of the Apocalypse." One night, without warning, hooded psychopaths set fire to his site. A few weeks later, they came back to extort money from him. He greeted them with a rifle. Straight out of the resistance fighter's manual. By the next day, he had set up the first patriot platoon in the region and had taken on the task of running the town hall, which the fundamentalists had burned down.

"I'm not disturbing you, I hope?"

"Not at all."

He pulls his robe fastidiously down over his navel.

"So?" he exclaims, his arm sweeping across the landscape. "Isn't it beautiful, this country? How can anyone live in such a hideous city, concrete everywhere, frightful tarmac, noise and pollution day and night?"

"By shutting your eyes and blocking your nose."

He leans on his elbow, resting his rifle along his leg, and looks around him.

"It was magnificent before. People used to come from all the neighboring villages on feast days. They would spread their blankets out and have picnics in peace. Kids would kick balls about. It was fabulous."

"We didn't know how lucky we were."

"You're right: we didn't know. There are people like that, who don't know how lucky they are."

"Nietzsche said, 'When peace reigns, the warlike man will make war on himself.'"

"Who's this Nitch?"

"One of our German cousins."

Arezki scours the length and breadth of his memory for this cousin, then gives up.

"By the way," he remembers suddenly, "your director left you a message at the post office. He wants you to go back."

"Is it urgent?"

"You're to report to Headquarters on Tuesday."

"That gives us four days to rustle up a visa," I say to Arezki.

"Speak for yourself. This time, the most powerful crane in the world wouldn't get me to budge from here…. Bab El-Oued is over for me. I want to die among my own people."

"You're right," agrees Akli enthusiastically. "The splendors of the ocean can't make the salmon forget the river where he was born."

❦

Akli has invited us to dinner at his home. He's invited everyone. In honor of the artists, he has hung up a portrait of Tahar Djaout between a pair of damascene swords. I was very fond of Tahar. He was a well-brought-up boy. If courtesy were to be made flesh one day, it would probably bear his face. Trained as a mathematician, but turning to journalism out of duty, he was also a talented poet. His worried eyes stare at me from his cast bronze frame, failing to understand what he is doing in a glass case, when he was born to conquer the world. He looks so out of place in there.... The finest Chinese vases can't console their flowers for the loss of their meadows.

Akli says, "Every time he came back to this country, he would always drop in on Igidher. He used to spend hours communing with the mountain. This is where he wrote his first prose."

I look at the deceased. With his handlebar moustache, he looks as though he is aping the high bohemian style of the black and white years. I find it hard to believe that the gun that ended his days didn't seize up in the face of such guilelessness. But in a land where infants are cut to pieces in their cradles, it would be offensive to barbarity to expect a response like that.

"Hey, Mister Mayor," says a chubby fellow with frizzy hair as he invades the hall. "You ought to keep your dogs tied up."

"I don't have any dogs."

"Where did this heap of shit in the street come from then?" he cries, pointing at a youth wearing camouflage gear in the courtyard.

"I'm not a heap of shit. Watch what you're saying, you idiot."

"It talks too! This place is obviously enchanted."

A shout of laughter applauds the entrance of this contumelious pair. The chubby one starts religiously kissing the old men on their turbans, deliberately missing out the *imam*....

"You've forgotten to kiss the sheikh's head," Mohand says reproachfully.

"He'd have to have one first."

"What do you mean, I'd have to have one first?"

"You hit a fake roadblock three times in a row. If you'd had one, the *khmej** *rouges* would have noticed."

Another salvo of laughter rings out.

The chubby one finishes his routine greetings, pours himself onto a padded bench and goes back to needling the youth, who has remained in the doorway, sullen and scowling.

"Hey, Rambo-on-a-diet. Is it true you picked up your paratrooper badge by falling out of a tree?"

"Yeah, falling out of your sister's bed, more like."

"Thanks for keeping me company. Now get lost. This place is for worthwhile people only."

Akli takes advantage of the general hilarity to growl in my ear: "Our very own Laurel and Hardy. The fat one's Bashir. He dropped out of Tizi Ouzou University to swell our ranks. In the resistance, he's as good as a steamroller, honest to God. Fear just isn't in his vocabulary. The little one's Amar. They're cousins and brothers-in-law. They keep up our troupe's morale. The militiamen love them."

A young man clears a passage through the tables and leans over the mayor. Akli frowns, nods and says,

"Of course, of course. Let them in."

The young man goes out into the courtyard and brings back a group of awestruck community guards in blue tunics.

"This is the Sidi Lakhdar patrol," Akli tells me. "They've just come back from a reconnaissance mission."

The community guards put their weapons down in a corner and mingle with the other guests.

Teenagers arrive bearing platters of grilled lamb, lettuce and onions. Bashir applauds and licks his lips.

"And now, let the Great Bellies begin!" he intones, echoing the magic words of a well-known television presenter.

༂

Mohand drives us back to Idir's house at about half past four in the morning, our heads ringing with jokes and laughter. Arezki couldn't

---

* *khmej*—garbage

take the pace. His long years of exile let him down. Half-asleep, he's swaying about in the back seat of the old car with its worn-out shock absorbers.

In the blue-tinged sky of the Naït-Walis, the crescent moon looks like a nail-clipping left behind by some kleptomaniac god. An opalescent gash in the folds of the horizon signals the miscarriage of another day. It's a beautiful night, and it's in full flight across the downy undulations of the land, while the wind, whether facetiously or merely undecided, wastes its time trying to unravel the clicking and whirring among the branches.

We cross the village's brightly illuminated main street, a thing of many colors thanks to its lights. Sliman's café is still open. Patriots sit at the tables, cigarettes between their lips and rifles on their laps. Here and there, clustered around the steps, teenagers add to the sweaty atmosphere, chatting or playing cards. People keep watch late at Igidher. Just in case.

The car plunges into an orchard, pursued by a pack of dogs. A shepherd sticks his head out through the half-open door of his hut. He recognizes the car and starts calming his animals down.

"We're going to build a school here," says Mohand. "Our children complain that the old one's too small. There'll be a playground and some showers too, as soon as we've fixed the water tower. That means the kids that like sport won't have to go to Sidi Lakhdar. We found a home-made forty-three-kilo bomb hidden under the road. An hour before the village bus was due to come by. Can you imagine the disaster if it had gone off? There were sixty schoolchildren on the bus. They were on an outing."

"You feel you can go on outings, the way things are?"

"You bet! We try to keep the kids' lives as close to normal as possible."

His hand grips the steering wheel hard.

"They weren't children, before. You should have seen them—huddled in corners, pale, shivering, shrieking the moment you looked at them. They were terrified animals. A car backfiring would send them into a frenzy. We couldn't possibly leave them in that state. They would have gone mad.... My own kid, he'd start blubbering any time I went into the next room to fetch something. He'd cling to my shadow day and night. We've gone through hell around here."

His tone lightens when we come out into a field:

"Here, there's going to be a youth club and maybe even a small stadium, with steps, and a stand for VIPs. We've got a lot of plans for the community. It's our way of taking up the challenge. We're rebuilding what fundamentalism has destroyed, and we're gaining ground every day. The best form of defense is always attack, that's what the captain told me."

The car bounces sharply into a crevasse. Mohand quickly swings the wheel round to avoid the ditch.

"You were right, Brahim. When you've got a problem, it's your problem. We must rely on ourselves first and foremost, and at the moment we're not doing too badly."

Idir's house rises up behind the trees, low and picturesque with its slate roof and cob walls.

I shake Arezki. The old painter jumps like a jack-in-a-box, struggles to find the door handle and can't even put a hand to it.

Mohand jumps down to the ground, hurries round to open his door and folds him in his arms.

"He's had it," I say to him. "It won't be long before we have to help him with his ablutions."

"The air of his beloved hillside will soon put him back on his feet, you'll see," Mohand promises, slipping his arms beneath the old man's limp body. "We'll take good care of him."

I turn on the light in the room.

Mohand puts his burden down on a pallet bed, takes off his shoes and covers him with a blanket.

"Nice shroud," I say grimly.

"If I were you, I'd do the same as him. I'd return to the fold with my wife and kids and draw a line under everything else.... Now, I have to leave. There're some snacks in the fridge and you'll find some spring water in the goatskin over there."

"You wouldn't have a couple of cigarettes? I used up my whole stock at the mayor's."

He hands me a pack of Ryms.

"Keep it…"

Suddenly, he goes over to the window and listens.

"What's that?"

He holds up his hand for silence. I listen out. Apart from the chirping and the occasional sighing of the breeze, I can't hear anything unusual.

Mohand goes out into the courtyard, climbs onto a heap of stones and peers into the distance, cupping his hand to his ear.

Far away, distorted by the somersaults of the wind, a crackle….

"Shots?"

"Sh!"

A single detonation, almost inaudible, then a short burst….

"Must be the Sidi Lakhdar patrol; they must have come across a band of terrorists."

"I just checked with the militiamen. The community guards returned to base at twenty past midnight."

The shots intensify, but it's impossible to tell where they're coming from in the darkness.

A truck arrives from the village, all its lights out.

Mohand takes a short cut to intercept it.

He comes back to me, pale.

"It's Akli's group. He's on his way to position 21."

"What happened?"

"Imazighen is under attack."

Icy water trickles down my back. Taos's slaughtered face burns in my soul. My knees sag and my heart pounds in my chest.

"Cowards!" I cry.

"Cowardice is Algerian. Bravery is Algerian. And there isn't room for both in the country. We're destined to follow the Devil all the way to hell."

He jumps into the car.

"Stay here, Brahim."

"No way."

The village is on full alert. The main road is deserted. Shadows move about on the roofs, taking up combat positions recognizable by the sandbags piled up on the terraces. On the road out of the village, searchlights sweep the surrounding fields. Streams of orders issue from the little houses, telling the women to keep calm.

Mohand leaves his car beside an irrigation cistern and joins his troupe, which is gathered, in formation, in a clearing.

An unimposing little man with red hair succinctly sums up the situation for us. "We don't know how many there are. We've taken up our positions. Bashir's holding position 18, Ramdan position 24. Within five minutes, Akli will seal off position 21."

"Very good."

Mohand inspects his men, checks their weapons and the first aid kit, tells an old man to get rid of his watch. He does so immediately.

"*They* won't get away this time."

The men nod, rigidly military. The men are brave, beautiful and mythical as only war can make them, to compensate for the wrong that will be done them in the minutes to come.

"Forward!"

The troupe moves as one man.

There's no question: if certain nations are still standing, it's not because their heads are held high but because their legs don't give way.

We're climbing the hill when there is a terrible explosion.

Down below, houses are on fire.

I am overcome by the sight. *Taos!* Without thinking, I hurl myself down the slope toward the village like a madman. A second explosion raises a monstrous plume of flames and dust. The upper wing of Imazighen is buried. The long-drawn-out lament of a machine gun rises over the few timorous bursts of fire from the village. Screams reach me in lacerating snatches. I run blindly, deaf to Mohand's calls. I feel my face being torn to shreds by the branches of the trees. *Taos!* I think I hear her voice among the shouts and rumbles; all I can see is her face in the flames of my nightmare. My foot hits an obstacle violently. I trip and tumble into a ditch.

Mohand catches up, beside himself:

"What's got into you? You can't run about like this in the dark.

You could get yourself shot by our own men. We have identification signals and strict orders."

The troupe proceeds in furtive spurts.

The red-haired guy asks whether we need a stretcher-bearer. We reassure him that we don't, and he hurries off in the direction of the skirmish.

Mohand helps me up.

"Are you sure you're okay?"

"Let's hurry up, or they'll be slaughtered."

We can now see sustained firing from the copse of trees overlooking the village. Tracer bullets chase each other along dotted lines of bright light. The screams of women and children pierce through the chorus of lead.

"The militiamen are on their way," the radio operator reports. "The captain is asking us to mark the way in."

"Akli can lead that. We'll have to be quick. The *khmej* will retreat and slip between our fingers."

We cut across the fields and through the barricades of cactus. Shots ring out nearby, on our left. Somebody drops behind me. It's the redhead. His shoulder has been torn off. He rolls to one side into some shelter. He hasn't made a sound.

Mohand climbs over toward him.

"Don't worry about me," whispers the redhead. "I'll be okay."

Suddenly, rising up out of eternity, a nightmarish shape attacks me with a thunderous *"Allahu akbar!"* an axe at the end of its arm. A burst of fire mows it down, and it collapses in front of me, mouth open and eyes staring. The horror! The monster has destroyed a cactus on its way down. He is a giant, at least a hundred and twenty kilos, with unending hair and a beard down to his navel. He looks like an ogre that has escaped from the jungle, or a werewolf, he's so utterly hideous. He stares at me with hatred in his eyes. His shoulders shake hungrily. He tries to get up, trembling alarmingly. His stench mesmerizes me, paralyzes me. A second burst of fire drops him to the ground. He sighs harshly. Threads of blood trickle from his mouth, and his head falls limply to one side.

When I come to, I see that Mohand's troupe is about to enter the first few houses of Imazighen. Somebody throws a grenade into a suspect courtyard. After the explosion, ten or so men attack while the remainder zigzag around, surrounding the hovels.

Signal lights flash at the top of a building. Mohand replies with his flashlight. We rush to the main square in a hail of machine-gun fire.

"They're pulling back, they're pulling back...."

"They're retreating into the woods...."

In the distance, the lights of the military convoy pierce the darkness.

Mohand notifies Bashir's group by radio and orders him to intercept the terrorists as they try to retreat toward him. Guns start hurling abuse at each other in the thickets again.

The burning houses illuminate the village as if it were broad daylight. There are two ragged corpses lying on the ground, their filthy beards fluttering in the wind. Another is scattered in pieces under a tree. The air is filled with the smell of cremated flesh. Behind a pall of ochre-hued smoke, a woman groans on the threshold of a house, her hands to her belly, trying to hold back the gushing blood. Civilians start emerging from their shelters, calling to each other in horror; others rush into the ruins to help the wounded.

An old man passes in front of us, hands held out like a sleepwalker. A patriot lifts him onto his shoulders and takes him to the main square. Women appear here and there, their children clutching their robes.

In a daze, I stare at the smoke roaring out of the ruins. Disemboweled beasts of burden sprawl in enormous pools of blood. Plumes of smoke dance in the crackling furnace.... Taos's home is totally destroyed. Only one wall is still standing, like a monument that has been struck by lightning. A truck, probably packed with explosives, has dug a tremendous crater in the courtyard. It has ended up overturned onto its cab, crippled, its chassis warped and the motor ripped out.

I go onto the devastated terrace as you might sink into madness. I feel as though I'm wandering in limbo. I'm just one shade among all the other shades of this disaster.... *Taos.... Taos....* Suddenly frantic,

I start pushing beams aside, lifting planks of wood, stones, scorching my hands on glowing rubble....

"Here I am," says a quavering voice behind me.

I turn, amazed.

She's there, just sitting on the stump of what was, a few moments ago, a magnificent carob tree. She's there, Taos, safe and sound, her brass chest in her hands.

"My father used to say: 'Go, Taos, you're a good girl. Wherever your feet may lead you, my *baraka** will be with you. You will be like a *houri*: you will see your enemies, but none of them will see you.'"

At that moment an agonizing pain shoots through my leg, and the ground disappears beneath me.

---

*   *Baraqa*: luck, good fortune

Chapter twelve

The boss is in his Sunday best when he welcomes me: novelty tie with satin-smooth shirt, Pierre Cardin suit, alligator shoes, freshly pressed hair, cheeks scrubbed pink. A joy to behold.

He's happy, and behaves like a person with great news to impart. In his boundless enthusiasm, he notices neither the cane with which I support myself nor my invalid state.

He spreads his arms wide and cries: "What a pleasure to see you again, Brahim. I thought you were avoiding me."

His joy is such that you almost want to take it at face value.

He invites me to relax in the leather sofa beneath the Algerian flag with its red star—a cozy little corner reserved for special visitors—and sits in the armchair beside me. His manicured hand ventures to pat my knee in a manner that means to be friendly but remains that of the head of the family mollifying the black sheep.

"Welcome aboard, superintendent. It's party time in the barracks."

"So I saw."

His glowing eyes make me uncomfortable.

He stands up abruptly:

"Tea or coffee?"

"Both."

He bursts out laughing.

"You'll never change, will you?"

"I might mistake myself for someone else."

"You're right…. So, how's the tribe?"

"It's paying the price of cosmopolitanism."

He raises an eyebrow.

When the boss doesn't understand, he raises an eyebrow. Knowing he's just a placeman, he's suspicious of anything he can't follow.

"But it will recover its investment."

"Well…."

He still doesn't get it. In fact, that's the good thing about him.

He rings for the guard, who appears presto.

"Tea and coffee for the prodigal son."

The guard bows down before me, submissive and compliant, giving me the gratification of showing how happy he is to see me again, and disappears with a swishing sound.

"Good old Aziz," says the boss with feeling. "He thinks the world of you."

I look at my watch meaningfully.

The director claps his hands happily, so happily….

"All's well that ends well, right, Brahim? One must never lose hope."

There's that word! Did I ever really have any? I don't think so. I used to believe in hope confidently and conscientiously, just as the aging mistress believes in the return of the lover who left one night to get some cigarettes and never came back. But I'm nobody's mistress. I've learned to be suspicious of the philosopher's carrots that dangle over the abyss. They're like the stale bread you hand out to the starving masses to make them think you care about them.

"I've never lost it, sir. You can't lose what you never had."

"Come on, Brahim. Don't spoil this splendid day."

"The day doesn't belong to me either."

My bitterness forces him back in his chair. He loses the thread and looks around for a counter-argument. His hand panics, and doesn't dare approach my knee. I have a vision of my lips, swollen with spite, my poisonous face, and I don't do a thing to remedy the situation.

"I understand," he says wearily. "We didn't do right by you, is that it? We were ungrateful and treacherous. But, Brahim, not everyone has it in him to distinguish between right and wrong. Sliman Houbel exceeded his authority. He's a megalomaniac. He thinks the rules don't apply to him, that he has a right to interfere in things that are none of his business. I'm here to tell you that many people disapproved of what he did. Some senior people put him firmly in his place. He tried to justify himself, of course. He went so far as to demand that you be brought up before a disciplinary board, on principle, to serve as an example to others who might be tempted to follow your example. I said no. And I wasn't the only one, believe me. We laid down our terms: Brahim Llob must be fully reinstated, both as a public servant and as a novelist. And we won. Not only do you get your old job back; you've even been nominated for the Police Medal."

I hiccup in vexation.

This time, the boss's hand strikes my thigh with some violence, "To hell with the Inquisition, Brahim. As far as I know, this isn't the Middle Ages any more. Algerians are dying—and in the worst possible ways—and it's not so that some comic-opera mandarins can walk all over us."

"Director," I break in, "I can never thank you enough for your support. I know you've busted a gut to get me back. It's just that a d'Erguez* is like a musket: once he's been fired, it's all over."

"You wouldn't do that to us...."

"Look, let's be rational for a moment. I'm limping toward sixty, I'm becoming the old guard; I'm more and more difficult to get along with. I've done my time; I have to give way to others. I'm tired of chasing after small-time hoods while the real bastards loll about, above

---

* *D'Erguez* (Kabyl dialect): "real" man

all suspicion. I'm not interested any more. I want to hang up my hat and go home. I've got kids I want to see up close, a bit more than before, a wife I'd like to distinguish from a beast of burden; maybe I can get them to forgive me for having sacrificed them for the sake of wrong-headed priorities. I want a rest, Mr. Menouar, I want to reacquaint myself with the simple things in life, shut myself up with a book for the whole day, maybe even travel…see the world. I'm sorry, I really am. I don't lack the desire, but my heart just isn't in it any more. Where I come from, in the mountains of the Naït-Wali, when a knight is thrown from his horse, he never gets back on."

Chapter thirteen

The nurse is very gentle. Nature has not blessed her with good looks, but she has a heart the size of a house. She's like a huge, old-fashioned wardrobe, barely dusted off from the antique store, with great folds of fat cascading from her shoulders down to her elbows and a massive, determined face. She pushes through the throng with the ease of an ice-breaker, greeted on her way by cheerful teasing.

"They love you here," I tell her.

"The feeling's mutual."

"You must be full to bursting."

"There isn't enough room in the other hospitals. They're packed in shoulder to shoulder. It's not comfortable, but it helps them stay on their feet."

The corridor is crammed with people, most of them victims of terrorist attacks. In a packed room, a young child allows himself to be amazed by an old doctor's conjuring tricks. He has a grotesque bandage around his head and an amputated leg. His little face shines like a ray of light in the surrounding chaos.

"There were eleven in the family," the nurse tells me. "He's the only one left, and even he's not unscathed. Within a few minutes he lost his father, mother, five sisters and three brothers. All massacred. He was struck with a machete on the head and again on the knee and was left for dead. He spent the night soaked in his family's blood. He hasn't said a word since. We try to keep him entertained. He joins in willingly, but it's just for show. In fact, his mind has retreated to the very depths of his being and refuses to come back up."

"No relatives?"

"We're still looking...."

One of the casualties, hopping about on a prosthetic leg, waves at me extravagantly.

"Hey! Superintendent...."

The man is tall and well built, with a ravaged face. He must be about thirty, but looks ten years older. The side of his face is caved in and his right eye is invisible. I try to place him, but in vain. He makes his way through the chaos as well as he can, visibly delighted to see me.

"Don't you recognize me? Wahab de Bir Mourad Raïs. I was in Lieutenant Chater's team."

"Ah!" I say, just to avoid upsetting him.

He plunges his clammy hand into mine. His smile fades.

"Molotov cocktail," he explains bitterly. "I didn't use to pay attention when people said 'nightfall.' It was just normal. Now, I know what it really means. Nights do fall, superintendent, just as men fall. And that makes a lot of noise in here," he adds, tapping his temple. "You hear it clearly, I can assure you.... One evening, when we were out on patrol, our armored car caught fire and rolled into a ditch. It was night that fell into the ditch. It's hard to explain. But I lived through it. My partners fell. One after another. They had no choice. Come out and be gunned down, or perish in the flames. They experienced both.... Choice: I know what that *really* means, now. It's no picnic...."

The nurse pinches me discreetly to let me know the guy is deranged. I'm helpless. I don't dare take my hand back, even though it's beginning to go numb, nor say a comforting word. The cop doesn't look as though he's expecting any sympathy. Like Malika Sobhi, he just wants people to be quiet when he's talking.

"Now, I pay more attention. Meanings have more subtlety. Words have profound significance...."

"That's good, Wahab," the nurse breaks in. "We'll talk about it later. I promise."

The injured man nods trustingly.

"Okay. We'll talk about it later. Promise?"

"You know I keep my word."

"That's true. You keep your word."

He frees my hand slowly, millimeter by millimeter.

"Wahab de Bir Mourad Raïs, Superintendent. You'll remember him...."

"I certainly will!"

"You'll mention him in your book. Wahab was dynamite. He was a fighter."

He stands to one side to let us pass.

I hear him calling himself all kinds of names behind my back, "Stop this circus act, Wahab. Or you really will go crazy. There are limits to everything, Wahab. Be careful.... Stop making people feel awkward. I warn you, I warn you...."

The nurse says, "He's not like this every day. It comes and goes. He has a guilt complex. He's the only survivor from that patrol."

We come out into the courtyard of the hospital. Lino is leafing through a magazine in the shade of a plane tree, his backside in a chair and his foot in plaster.

"He's adorable," the nurse confides. "And hilarious. He has steel in his spine."

I thank her.

She crushes my fingers between hers and goes back to her patients.

Lino shuts his magazine, pushes his glasses back and notices my stick.

"War wound or dog turd?"

"War...."

"Good. We're even. When did you get back?"

"Last night."

He grimaces in an exaggerated manner and moves his leg. He

117

looks well. It's as if he's grown up, or perhaps it's just the fledgling moustache that gives that impression. I ruffle his hair. He shies away from my condescending gesture. I know how much he hates anyone touching his hair, which is cut in a style taken from an advertisement for hair products, but I've always taken mischievous pleasure in winding him up.

"So, what about this sprain?"

"It's not a sprain."

"Is it serious?"

"The doc reckons, if you can teach monkeys to ride bikes, it must be possible to teach their descendants to use wheelchairs."

And then, to reassure me, "Nothing really bad. In a few weeks, I should be able to kick some parliamentary pachyderm up the ass without difficulty."

"It'll take much more than that to drive him out of his seat.... I brought you some Swiss chocolate."

"Thanks."

He puts the bar of chocolate on the table. His face goes soft. He's worried about something.

I sit down in front of him and read, one by one, among the drawings and obscure inscriptions on the plaster, a list of girls' names.

"Your conquests?"

"I like people to think I'm still getting laid, even though I'm laid up in bed."

Lino is more than worried: he's unhappy. I guess that he's trying to undo the present fatal turn of events. His efforts are doomed, and he knows it. He understood as soon as he saw me. He just refuses to face facts. He slides his finger nervously over his moustache and picks furiously at a spot in the corner of his mouth. A couple of sparrows land near us, play at the foot of the tree, then swoop vertiginously back up into the sky.

Lino clears his throat, hesitates and then says, "Ewegh told me some great news.... I hope you're not here to blow it out of the water."

"I'm sorry."

He throws his head back. In a spotless sky, the two sparrows catch each other, split up, chase each other and join up again amid the dazzling light of the day. Lino purses his lips. After an interminable silence, he gulps, "I couldn't be sure. When someone has more pride than common sense...."

"In any case, there's no room for either any more."

He looks evasively up at the top of the plane tree, the walls of the compound, the invalids wandering about on the burning dirt of their suffering. He clenches his fist. A few tables away, a transistor radio plays some *hawzi* music, filling the air with its deep melancholy.

"There's...no chance of a change of heart?"

"This isn't a spur of the moment thing, Lino. I've thought about it, gone over the data from all possible and conceivable angles...."

He bangs his fist on the arm of his chair.

"Damn! The place is going to the dogs...."

"Don't say that. Good men will leave; better ones will replace them...."

"Now you're talking like a damned politician...."

"Listen to...."

"Stop.... Please, don't say any more. You've said your final word. That's good enough, I assure you."

"Lino...."

"Lino what? You don't have to justify yourself. You've decided to hang up your hat. That's your right. The rest is just hypocrisy. And besides, who am I to judge you? Who am I? Can you tell me? You have your reasons, that's obvious. You're free to respond to them any way you want. But don't you think it would be kinder on the rest of us to keep them to yourself? It would be more honest, fairer.... The others, they don't give a damn. They don't count."

He slips his crutch under his arm, firmly rejects my help and gets up. His lips are trembling. He realizes his words don't match up to his emotions, but decides not to throw them in my face. He's so angry with me that he pretends to forget about the Swiss chocolate I bought for him. He doesn't turn round once as he walks toward a big gate at the end of the courtyard.

Chapter fourteen

They're all here: friends, sympathizers, incorrigibles, complainers.... They jostle for front-row seats, some to get a good view, others to score points over those who are not there. The big lecture theater in the basement at Headquarters is packed. It's a historic moment. The demystification of a legend is about to be witnessed, the sealing up of a big mouth, the discharge of an indiscreet, recidivist superintendent of police.

Even Haj Garne is here. The price, for him, is absenting himself from his coterie of screaming dykes and insatiable queens, but he has come. He wouldn't miss it for the world. He strokes his long thin snout shiftily, lubricating his preserved-aspic smile over and over again with his blue-green tongue. He's in seventh heaven, which is quite an achievement for an old devil who is more accustomed to the pestilential depths of the gutter.

He shudders with an orgasm on a seismic scale when I catch his eye. Beside him, Sofian Malek quivers with happiness. This delightful piece of garbage is a nephew of Ghoul's:* a vulgar paranoiac

---

* See *Morituri* by Yasmina Khadra, *The* Toby Press, 2004

who shoots up with insulin, continually undoing an imaginary tie ever since a failed suicide attempt in his youth, when he tried to hang himself from a clapped-out ceiling light. He, too, has come to see with his own eyes the official discharge of the most notorious cop in the city, even if it means keeling over from hyperglycemia. His nostrils flare as I approach him. His lips chew me up and curse me. His protruding eyes follow my movements everywhere, ferocious as Nessus' shirt. At this moment, he wishes he could be the unleashed thunderbolt of heaven, the destructive fury of a freak who more or less believed he could bring the gods to their knees until an ordinary farmyard pig came and brought his Olympus down like a house of cards.

"It's the museum for you, you old whore!" he whispers to me at point-blank range.

"I'm right where I belong," I reply: "in *your* nightmares. I'll spend every night torturing you in your sleep. It'll be so horrible you won't want to shut your eyes."

"We'll see about that, mister *former* policeman."

"The sooner the better."

We are eyeball to eyeball, nose to nose, breath to breath. His grin withers and frantic tics spread all over his playboy face.

"Come on, we don't talk to corpses," says Haj Garne soothingly.

"That's right," Sofian agrees, a hair's breadth away from imploding. "What you do with carrion is piss on it to freshen it up."

I go on my way, with a nauseating aftertaste in my mouth.

I recognize some friendly faces in the audience. They are moved, so I'm not the only one. Ewegh is standing stiffly at the end of the first row, his chin up. His eyes are riveted on the stage, aloof and taciturn as a lizard atop his *barkhan*.* On his right, Lino musters what's left of his dignity. His dark red Yves Saint-Laurent suit, a fake, marks him out as the bachelor-about-town that he is. Now that he's rid of his plaster, he looks as though he wants to kick the whole world's ass. He turns his head discreetly in my direction and immediately turns away, but not quickly enough to hide the glistening light in his eyes.

---

* *Barkhan*: crescent-shaped dune

My secretary, Baya, manages to shrink into her handkerchief, her nose red. I give her a wink to cheer her up: no good. Her shoulders hunch convulsively and she starts sobbing again.

Omar Rih welcomes me at the foot of the scaffold. He's in charge of protocol. He's a charming fellow, oozing with exaggerated consideration. If you ask him for a glass of water, he'll bring you the spring in the palm of his hand. If you advise him to keep his cool, he'll descend into a state of hypothermia without hesitation.

He grips me warmly by the hand and shows me up onto the platform.

Mourad Smaïl doesn't offer the smallest grimace to my person. I suppose his rank and his personal fortune make it unnecessary for him to consider underlings. He's the overall boss of the police. His very name causes trauma. Wherever his presence is announced, there's an instant shortage of tranquillizers. Hated like sin, and you wouldn't believe how he's feared. Never content. Constantly trying to catch his yes-men out and always looking for lice on hairless heads, on the pretext that you can't necessarily see through ideas that are too clear. A megalomaniac of unusually humble origins, who came from nowhere—to be precise, a dirty little office reserved for feeble nobodies and ripe for reform—to find himself, thanks to some mischievous sprite, the officially mandated mentor of a formidable army which he lashes like a domestic animal.

My revered father, a *qadi** by profession and a well-read philosopher, used to say: "There's no worse tyrant than a spittoon-emptier turned sultan." I should have spent more time listening to him.

Mourad Smaïl is not the only one on the platform, though it would be wiser not to mention the fact—wherever Mourad Smaïl is, he's reluctant to allow room for even God the Father—but here he's surrounded by a band of replete Buddhas, strictly limited to walk-on parts, who are abusing their position by taking a nap, their eyelids almost down to their lips and their hands resting solemnly on their bellies, which gives their affected asceticism that air of post-prandial nonchalance so dear to do-nothing kings.

*   *Qadi:* Islamic magistrate

A little apart, back in his role of doormat, Hadi Salem tries to be a carbon copy of his boss. He sniffs whenever the latter blows his nose, scratches his chin in the same way he does, and watches religiously to make sure none of his own deeds or gestures exceed or diminish those of the towering presence before him.

Omar Rih offers me a seat at the end of the table. The director slips a hand under the table to feel me up amiably. A happy life is a hidden life. The director keeps his life well hidden.

Mourad Smaïl takes a swig from a glass of mineral water—Hadi Salem, behind him, gulps—and taps the microphone twice. The noise dies down. The people in front turn toward the people at the back to tell them to listen up. A profound silence falls. A fly starts buzzing in the hush.

"Okay," blares Mourad Smaïl without any ado. "Fanfares are not my favorite thing, nor are song-and-dance acts. *I* call a spade a spade. I'll get right to the point: I'm disappointed!"

The Buddhas around him shake their heads contritely.

"I find it particularly unpleasant to bid farewell to a colleague at a time when the security situation demands everyone's total mobilization."

There are a few muted groans of protest at the back of the hall, quickly silenced by the indignant shushing of the front rows.

Mourad Smaïl wipes his maw with a Kleenex while sweeping the impudent stalls with a threatening eye. Calm returns, along with the fly.

"I'm no diplomat," he thunders. "I was brought up hard and inflexible. That has its consequences, but it forges a man. That's the way I am," he clarifies, chopping the air with an invisible meat-cleaver.

In the front rows, throats are cleared and necks disappear into shoulders.

"When you get off a moving train, you risk leaving some flesh on the tracks. Superintendent Llob knows this. So he won't be expecting any eulogies from me."

I'm stunned.

What strikes me most, in this mass of fat and pathological arrogance, is not the incredible authority he wields, and not his disarming self-confidence, which earns him the *baraka* traditionally bestowed upon ogres cast in his mould; what strikes me right away is the way his face shows no sign of ever having been touched by the shadow of a doubt or a regret: it's a face modeled on a totem, the forehead more prominent than the goitre projecting from the neck, featuring a pair of annihilating eyes and an absolutely monstrous mouth; a catalyst face in which the power of evil and the pathological need to exercise it are combined, as if the only way to make your presence felt were to terrorize your world before wiping it out in a stream of spittle.

"Superintendent Llob is leaving us. That is deplorable. Yet it's not the end of the world. Algeria is not subject to the menopause. Fortunately, fortunately, God be thanked."

He pauses, shoos away a fly, pouts at his glass of water. In front of him, foreheads sweat and eyes shift.

"I won't spend much time on his career. We're paid to do our jobs. Nobody expects charity from us. I believe each of us is aware of what he does. Each of us is responsible to his colleagues and to history.

"Our nation recognizes her own. Full stop, new paragraph.... I take the opportunity of this 'gathering' to remind those who have a tendency to forget it that the war is not over, and that there's no chance of winning it by running away...."

The Buddhas nod piously.

"The superintendent isn't twenty any more. Nor is he the only one. He has decided it's the right moment to retire from the chase. That's his right. He has his reasons, though some will think he's wrong. Either way, it's up to nobody but him.... To bring things to a close, I do not wish him good luck. He's just given up on luck. I wish him courage, because retirement is not a sinecure for men who carry phantoms around with them...."

He swallows some water and says, "Over to you, Mister Menouar, and please try to keep it short."

The director is pale. He wasn't expecting such a patched-together, rushed speech. He's taken aback, and the speech he has transferred onto three sheets of fine paper suddenly seems impossible, less plausible than an alchemist's formula.

"If you please, Mister Menouar," says Mourad Smaïl impatiently.

The director recovers from his cataleptic state with difficulty. He staggers to the podium and fiddles awkwardly with the microphone until Omar Rih comes to his rescue. Then he gets all tangled up in a vain hunt for a handkerchief, gives up and becomes absorbed in his now burdensome and useless papers. The vise-like silence becomes more oppressive and makes him anxious. He clears a reluctant frog from his throat, breathes in, breathes in again and starts speaking in a shaky voice, "The Director General of Police is right not to dwell on Superintendent Llob's career. That task, thankless though it may be, should logically fall to me."

He is breathless. He is flustered. He concentrates. He consults his innermost soul, looking to extract the vein of courage he gave up years ago in order not to upset the sensibilities of a hierarchy that was accustomed to total submission and the dyed-in-the-wool humility of flunkeys. The director is aware of the dangers he is courting. I can feel him painfully climbing the steps to his own scaffold, his rock of Sisyphus in front of him, but he hangs on and, bit by bit, climbs the mountain of his uncertainty. His forehead dripping, his throat dry, he searches for words amid the tumult. His hands are damp with the strain of being the focus of everybody's attention; his veins are bulging under the weight of everyone's eyes. He breathes in again, and again, looks up for help, meets my eyes. I smile at him and, as if by magic, he frees himself from the baking hothouse of fear and says, "It is very presumptuous to judge others. We should, instead, be their equals, deserve to lead them, deserve their obedience and confidence. Being the boss is supposed to mean that you have something more than others, some wisdom perhaps, more dedication, more perception; something definitely superior that would justify their agreeing to carry out the most absurd orders, not to whine, to tolerate a few excesses on somebody's part even though the regulations and convention might frown on them. With Brahim, this wasn't easy to do. He has been under my command for nigh on ten years, and we haven't always had a relaxing relationship. We've shouted each other hoarse many times, and we've had several periods of not speaking to each other. I can't say he hasn't had a part in the white hairs on my head.... I've been hauled over the coals because of him. And what does it all leave...? A goodbye speech I'm having to improvise on the fly because the one I wrote yesterday is already stale....What can you say about superintendent Llob now, in the heat of the moment, knowing the risk of saying something clumsy or expressing some disillusionment? Will my words measure up to his deeds? I don't think so.... So I'd be grateful if you forgave me for not measuring up to the moment either....

"Was Brahim a good policeman? I think so. A difficult subordinate, but an outstanding policeman. Was he right to favor one over the other, or was he wrong? One thing's for sure: he obeyed his conscience, and that's not something to be taken for granted. While Algeria was desperately trying to find herself, among all the twists and turns and all the searchlights, while everyone else was fighting for a place in the sun, Brahim walked a straight line. Mouth-watering temptations, profit, the soft option—they never attracted him. And he'll never be forgiven for that either. Brahim steered a course toward what he considered loyal and right; the rest didn't matter much. He set out his itinerary before he left, and he followed it his whole life, courageously and with self-denial. Today, he doesn't regret it one bit. He has *succeeded*. He and his conscience are in harmony, which is not—alas!—the case for a good many of us....What can you say about a man who embraced a career in the Force just so as to be a defender of order, who believed in justice and equity with all his might and who worked like a dog to be their worthy servant, while others shamelessly abused them, flouting the most basic rules of propriety?... Nothing. You say nothing. You sit quietly and watch. Modesty demands that you sit quietly in the face of righteousness. Especially when you lack it yourself."

He turns to me and looks at me intently. His eyes are shining, and the sheets of paper are rustling in his restless hands, "Brahim, my friend, if there's anyone who deserves to be a Cop, with a capital letter the size of an obelisk, it's you."

The back of the hall erupts in a deafening ovation. The euphoria spreads gradually to the front rows and then, like a tidal wave, to the platform. One of the Buddhas stands up suddenly, still clapping fit to scorch his palms. One after the other, rows of people stand up amid the din echoing around the hall. Lino nudges Ewegh in the ribs to wake him up and winks at me. Baya's ululations ring out, clear as a rushing stream. The director spreads his arms out to me, despite Mourad Smaïl's scowling visage. I stand up and embrace him amid delirium from the hall.

"Thank you," I mumble. "Thank you. I'm deeply touched."

⁂

After the ceremony, Lieutenant Chater and his team of Ninjas* insisted on taking some souvenir pictures with me in the courtyard at Headquarters. Other companions in arms join us there to congratulate me and express condolences. Captain Berrah,† of the Security Services' Communications Center, who missed the main event because his car broke down, catches up with me just as I'm about to say goodbye. His flatfish face is hidden behind sunglasses, which is reassuring. The evidence of Ewegh's false move is on its way to becoming a distant memory, because the flattened nose is growing back. First, he has his picture taken with me too, then between Lino and the Touareg, thus burying a pointless hatchet.

Inspector Bliss turns up on tiptoe, smiling uncertainly. He waits patiently while the photographer readies his equipment, then plants himself in front of me. His rodent-like paw fiddles with a pin in the national colors in his lapel.

"Now that you're slipping between my fingers, *superintendent*, I suppose I'll have to make do with someone else."

It's the first time he's called me this.

He's moved.

"You were my favorite victim," he adds, his voice cracking.

He removes the pin from his lapel and pins it to my chest.

"My son gave it to me on the fifth of July. Today, I'm giving it to you. I don't take pride in having a place in your heart. I'll be con-

---

* Algerian Special Forces
† See *Double Blank by* Yasmina Khadra, *The* Toby Press, 2004

tent with a square centimeter on your chest. That's enough to make me happy, I promise you."

He puts his hands on my shoulders and embraces me furtively.

"I'm going to miss you."

And then he flees, unable to hold back his emotion.

As he disappears sadly through the crowd, I wonder whether our enmity wasn't ultimately just due to a simple misunderstanding, to the troublesome problem of communication.

Lino suggests we continue the party at Rimmel, a high-class restaurant on the waterfront. I explain to him how badly I need to just kick about in the streets. It's a beautiful day, and a quiet conversation with my own shadow would do me good. He doesn't insist, but promises to come and see me at home later in the evening.

"Try to not to get drunk beforehand."

"I'll try…."

I leave through a door hidden behind some ivy, fetch my car from the garage and drive around all morning, wherever the road takes me. At noon, I retire into a bistro at the foot of the Maqam monument. I wolf down three *merguez* sandwiches and smoke at least half a dozen cigarettes, then have a strong coffee on the terrace at the Oasis, in the shade of a rainbow-colored umbrella.

At around three o'clock, I walk down to the Moutonnière and watch a bunch of bums squabbling. Their unintelligible shouts spew out among the waves before blending into the open sea, drowned out by the sound of the Mediterranean. The sea is in a trance. It launches its troops at the coast, tries to scatter the rocks, comes and goes in a series of gestures that fool nobody. One of these days I'll buy some fishing rods and go out on the jetty to catch fish. I'll put on a hat to protect me from the sun and shoot the breeze with my kids the whole day long. Mina will watch me tirelessly casting my hooks out as far as I can; every move will bear, in her eyes, the hallmark of great prowess. Afterwards, we'll grill our catch on the beach. When evening falls, it will be hard to part from our dreams.

A passerby asks me the time. Strangely, my watch has stopped at three thirty-five. I sling my jacket over my shoulder and walk back up into town. I walk along the sea front, across Bab El-Oued and the kasbah and return to my car, which is parked in Place des Martyrs. Algiers is like a darkroom sometimes: a single ray of light could spoil everything. I remember Serdj, beheaded at a fake roadblock on a no-go road; remember his kid, who was chasing an old bicycle wheel and couldn't understand why there were so many people at his house. As I sigh, a wrecked bar shows me its ruined walls. Home-made bomb. A school reminds me that they opened fire on children no more than knee-high. A porch tells me the story of that young conscript who will never know the joy of demobilization. How many dramas along my way, how many serious misunderstandings....

I remember the first time I trod the tarmac of Algiers. It was a Friday. The rattling bus that "transferred" me from Igidher via Ghardaïa parked in Place Premier Mai at the very moment the *muezzin* issued the call to *dhor*. I left my briefcase on the steps of the mosque. After prayers, my briefcase was still there, pushed slightly to one side to clear the way to the hall. It was 1967, a time when you could spend the night wherever it overtook you, without worrying about your wallet, never mind your life.

Spring excelled itself that Friday. The balconies were covered in blooms and all the girls, dressed up in their flowing milk-white robes, smelled like meadows. It was a time when chance took its inspiration from the days God made—happy days. The streets led me along their happiness, spreading drugstores, shop windows, barbecues and squares before me; and I, cocky peasant that I was, uncomfortably clothed in my broadly striped Tergal suit that resembled a convict's tunic, my shirt collar projecting stiffly over the collar of my jacket, would spend hours strutting about, proud of my cowboy belt with its buckle in the design of a huge medallion struck with a pair of silver Winchesters. I fell in love with the slightest smile, every time I learned a woman's first name. With my fresh-faced country boy face and my newly promoted inspector's stripes, I was ready to conquer hearts and minds. I was twenty-eight years old and had every reason to believe I owned the place.

And one day, just as I was declaring myself the lover of the whole city, I met Mina. At a dry cleaner's, right in the heart of the kasbah. I had come to borrow a tie for my Saturday night. She was there, waiting to pick up her father's *burnous*.* It was a magical moment of extreme intensity. Sequestered behind her white veil, fearful of my depraved glances, she tried to reject me with her eyes, as young women of good family were supposed to do; she had enormous eyes with infinite power to bewitch. Ever since, at the break of dawn, at the climax of every fireworks display, I see those eyes again, so beautiful that I am convinced that the love of a woman, all by itself, magnifies one's love of the whole world.

And what is left today of the Algiers of yesteryear…?

When considering the Algerian tragedy, history will remember the drifting of a people who compulsively chose the wrong guru, and the opportunism of a band of monkeys who, having no family tree, got into the habit of manufacturing breadfruit trees and gibbets for themselves in a country that will have excelled while of unsound mind.

It was eleven o'clock by the time Lieutenant Lino arrived at Rue des Frères-Mostefaï. The pavements were crowded with people. The lights on the police cars were revolving slowly in the darkness, running their blue light over the facades of the buildings. Families were watching the activity below from their balconies, amid an intolerable silence.

"What is it now?" grumbles Lino as he parks his car apprehensively to one side.

An officer gestures to him to go back where he came from. Lino shows him his badge.

"What's going on?"

Without waiting for a reply, he gets out of his car, walks toward the crowd, gradually speeding up as he gets closer to the center of events, finally starting to run, with his heart bursting.

---

* *Burnous*: robe

He pushes the onlookers aside, jostles them, forces his way to the front of number 51. The sight that greets his eyes brings him up short.

"It's not true," says Lino incredulously as the ground threatens to disappear from under his feet.

The man lying on the ground is Inspector Llob. His eyes are turned back, his mouth is gaping wide open and his chest is horribly mutilated.

Lino steps around him and leans against a wall so as not to collapse. His legs give way; he slides slowly into a sitting position, takes his head in his hands and falls to his knees.

Vaguely, he hears someone tell the story:

"Somebody shot him from a car heading this way. They just emptied their magazines into him. He didn't stand a chance."

About the Author

Yasmina Khadra

Yasmina Khadra is the pseudonym of Mohammed Moulesse-houl, an Algerian army officer born in 1956, who adopted a woman's pseudonym to avoid military censorship. Moulessehoul held a high rank in the Algerian army, and despite the publication of several successful novels in Algeria, only revealed his true identity in 2001, after going into exile and seclusion in France. He is uniquely placed to comment on vital issues of the Middle East, Algeria, and fundamentalism. Newsweek acclaims him as "one of the rare witnesses capable of giving a meaning to the violence in Algeria today."

Khadra's previous books, *In the Name of God*, *Wolf Dreams*, *Morituri*, and *Double Blank*, have also been published in English by *The* Toby Press.

The fonts used in this book are from the Garamond family

Other works by Yasmina Khadra
also available from *The* Toby Press

In the Name of God

Wolf Dreams

Morituri

Double Blank

The Toby Press publishes fine writing,
available at leading bookstores everywhere. For more
information, please visit www.tobypress.com